Wrapped up in her own personal problems and fears, fourteen-year-old Jimmie Gavin does not see the growing strains in her parents' relationship. And she is completely unprepared for the breakdown of their marriage. The divorce changes Jimmie's family life and her feelings about her parents, and forces her to reevaluate and try to understand the difficulties that each member of her family has to face.

One of today's most distinguished and versatile writers, Mary Stolz has written more than thirty-five books for young adults and children. The *Atlantic Monthly* called her "one of the most rewarding writers for teen-agers." Among her books are *The Bully of Barkham Street, A Dog on Barkham Street,* and *In a Mirror,* all available in Yearling editions, and *Good-By My Shadow* and *Who Wants Music On Monday?,* both available in Laurel-Leaf editions. Ms. Stolz was born in Boston, grew up in New York City, and now lives in Stamford, Connecticut.

The Laurel-Leaf Library brings together under a single imprint outstanding works of fiction and nonfiction particularly suitable for young adult readers, both in and out of the classroom. This series is under the editorship of Charles F. Reasoner, Professor of Elementary Education, New York University.

LEAP BEFORE YOU LOOK

Mary Stolz

Published by
Dell Publishing Co., Inc.
1 Dag Hammarskjold Plaza
New York, New York 10017

FOR TOM AND ROBERT

The sense of danger must not disappear:
The way is certainly both short and steep.
However gradual it looks from here;
Look if you like, but you will have to leap.

W. H. AUDEN

CHAPTER ONE

The afternoon sun, reflecting off snow through the many-paned windows of the morning room, made the lights on the Christmas tree so pale that Jimmie Gavin, coming in to tidy up the morning's disarray, wasn't sure the tree was still lit. She moved closer, peering a little.

Yes, the lights were on, but too weak to rival that bright snow light flashing across the field behind the house.

She sighed a little, looking at the ornaments. They got to be such a part of your life, coming out each year for a couple of weeks, then going back into hiding. Some forgotten but then instantly recalled, and some looked for eagerly as the crumpled tissue-paper packets were undone to reveal—ah, the swan with tarnished tinsel tail, the pear-shaped ball encrusted with glitter, the tiny wooden birds with wire legs that Jimmie's father had carved and painted long ago. The string of lights made up of little gingerbread men. She could remember seeing the swan, the little birds, the glowing gingerbread men as long as she could remember seeing anything.

Those, and some others, went as far back as her parents' childhood Christmas trees. When they had got their divorce, last summer, it had seemed to Jimmie that they divided up their possessions in such a one-for-you-one-for-me way that she had almost expected them to take their two children and say, "You have that one and I'll

have this one." But no—she and her brother had remained with their mother, and so had the Christmas decorations. Maybe, because it was summer, her father
hadn't remembered about them.

And Mother, Jimmie thought, aiming for sarcasm and
missing, wasn't about to call anything to his attention.

"The fact is," Mrs. Gavin had said to her husband
with an air of bitter detachment, "you shouldn't get any
of the household things. Those, in most cases, go to the
wife."

"Is that a tradition of divorce? I hadn't known."

"You know now. I'm only giving you your mother's
things because I don't want them. But if I did want them,
there'd be nothing you could do. You'll get your divorce.
That should be enough for you."

"I get the divorce, you get the family silver, is that it?"

"If that's the way you choose to put it."

There'd been scenes like that, lots of them, mostly
conducted when they thought the children were out, or
asleep. But even if we'd never actually heard, Jimmie
thought, we'd have known how they were talking to each
other, even if we didn't know exactly what they were saying.

She studied the tree again, giving it her full attention.
Yards of cranberry ropes and popcorn strings that she
and her mother and Goya had made for days before
Christmas. It was one of the few activities her normally
inactive mother engaged in—decorating for a feast. For
as long as Jimmie could remember, her mother had made
valentines with her, had laid out Easter-egg hunts. She
had carved grinning jack-o'-lanterns and put them on the
front porch where their candle smiles glimmered in the
dark. And every Christmas she strung yards and yards
and yards of cranberry and popcorn necklaces for the
tree. As Jimmie got older, she found something wistful
about all this.

This year there were quite a lot of new plastic ornaments, bought by Grandmother Prior, even though Mom
didn't like them. She liked the old-timey kind that were
apt to break and had faded decorations on them. But
Grandmother, in some ways less counterclockwise, more

with it than her daughter, had bought this enormous tree (the morning room was much bigger than the living room they'd had at home) and they didn't have enough stuff left from the old life to fill it up. So—plastic junk.

She leaned over and pulled the electric cord from its socket. All at once the tree seemed not only to darken still more, but to grow smaller.

Christmas afternoon was a drag. Even at the old house, Jimmie had never liked Christmas afternoon. And it wasn't because there were no more presents to open, either. There was something else. A feeling of the end of something, except it didn't end marvelously, like a firework that exploded in light and disappeared. It ended like a bit of damp balloon busted at the end of a string.

("Burst, dear," she could hear her grandmother say. "The word, Janine, is burst.")

She began to poke aimlessly at the boxes and wrappings and ribbons, gaudy leftovers from the morning's gift-giving, which she had been instructed to clear up.

"Christmas afternoon is a drag and it always has been," she muttered aloud, trying to put the blame for how she felt on the day, on the time of the day. But she knew it wasn't that. And it wasn't because she wouldn't be seeing Julian today, either. She was pretty sure she was in love with Julian. She thought of him in the morning when she woke and at night before she went to sleep and most of the day in between. Who had said that to her once, about love, about loving? Anne, probably. Anne was the one who was always in love. *Jimmie—that is, Janine— loves Julian.* She'd be willing to declare it in an open meeting. Well, maybe not. She'd be willing to declare it to Julian, though, and one day might, one day almost surely would. But would wait, of course, for him to declare first, because Julian was that kind of boy. Old-fashioned, you'd have to call him. And herself, too, probably. In some ways. Not all.

But it wasn't missing Julian for just one day that was making her hurt and heartsick now, hollow inside with longing. Sitting amid the littering glitter, the chaos of holiday wrappings, she thought back to last Christmas, in their old house, when her mother and father had still been married and any other possibility would have seemed as unbearable as death itself. Well, it hadn't turned out to be unbearable. In a sad, awfully real sense she was happier now than she'd been when she was struggling against the realization that her parents *did not like each other*, struggling not to know that her father, who loved her, was going to make a life without her anyway.

CHAPTER TWO

On Christmas, a year ago, Goya had come into her room at five o'clock and gently tugged at the pillow on her head.

"You there, Jimmie?" he whispered.

"Under the bed. Look and you'll see."

Giggling, he yanked the pillow from her enfolding arms. "You're silly. People sleep on top of pillows, not under them."

"Well, I'm different. And I'm asleep. Give me back my pillow."

"Jimmie, it's snowing!"

"It is?"

She sat up eagerly and sure enough, in the night, while they slept, the longed-for snow had begun. Already it was beginning to sift up the corners of the windowpanes and outside it was falling thickly.

"Goya!" she shouted with delight. "You *did* it. It snowed after all."

"I told you it would," he said modestly. "Or else Santa Claus couldn't ride through the sky. It always snows for Santa. And," he went on, "I went down and looked, and he ate his cookie and drank the milk. So there. I didn't peek at the tree," he added. "I closed my eyes and *backed* in and then turned on the light when I could only look at the fireplace." He wanted to be quite clear about this, as he'd promised his sister not to look at the Christmas tree until they could see it together. Jimmie loved to watch his face at that moment.

Now she looked helplessly at this brother of hers who had contrived to reach the age of five still believing in Father Christmas, in witches streaking across the moon with cats perched on their broomsticks, in the Easter Bunny and the Tooth Fairy, in scarecrows dancing across fields when the moon was full and snowmen coming to life when the night was dark.

One time he'd told his sister that the Holy Grail was crossing the sky. Jimmie had looked out the window and seen the red and green lights of a small airplane passing overhead.

"What do you know," she'd said, while the rapt Goya had leaned on the window seat and said, "Just like in King Arthur, Jimmie. The Holy Grail. Up in the sky."

What could she have done? A little brother smart enough to remember all the King Arthur stories she'd read to him—smart enough to want them read to him— and dumb enough to believe they were for real. What did you do with a kid like that?

While Goya gazed at a vision, Jimmie had settled for, "What do you know," as she now settled for a nod, and therefore acceptance of Santa Claus plunging down the chimney and joyfully discovering refreshments on the hearth.

I suppose, she thought uneasily, we ought to tell him sometime. Only, not yet. Having made this cheerful decision, she got out of bed, pulled on her robe, and agreed with Goya to go downstairs to look at the tree and open their stockings, which they were allowed to do no matter what time they woke up on Christmas morning.

"You stay back," she whispered to him, so as not to wake their parents or their father's mother, Gram, whose turn it was to visit for the holidays. "I'll plug in the lights for you. Now, *wait*."

She turned on the wall switch and looked around the living room. It was abnormally neat and clean because Gram was a compulsive housekeeper. At least, that was what her daughter-in-law called her. "Go ahead, clean away," young Mrs. Gavin would say. "*I* don't get my feelings hurt at the implication that I'm a slob." And then, of course, Gram would slow down, or work on shelves and closets, things that didn't show.

The tree was in a corner, surrounded by gifts, most of them wrapped, except that Goya's first small two-wheeled bicycle and a toboggan for Jimmie were dazzlingly open to view. When the lights of the tree went on, Goya caught his breath at its beauty, and Jimmie caught her at the sight of his pure and single-hearted joy.

A rather small but very shapely tree it was, spreading spangled branches, filling the air with that special odor that was foresty and homey at the same time.

Goya, in a daze, looked from the tree to the bicycle and back.

"Isn't it beautiful, Jimmie?" he said at last. "Isn't it the best beautiful you've ever seen?"

Jimmie looked around the shabby room, at the tree and the bike and the toboggan, then out to the snow falling steadily, whitely in the dark. She smiled, and sighed happily. "It sure is, darling. The best."

Gram came down, already dressed, while they were looting their stockings. The rest of them always spent Christmas morning in their bathrobes. It was part of the tradition of Christmas morning, as were carols and Gregorian chants and medieval string music on their father's stereo system. As was a breakfast deliberately, teasingly, prolonged by their father, who would finally consent to take his coffee to the living room and so allow the revels to begin.

But his mother, Gram, on her year to visit, always came downstairs fully dressed, even wearing an apron, so that she could get breakfast started. She was plump and pink-skinned and wore gold-rimmed glasses and had grandmother-colored hair. She was perfectly glad to call Janine Jimmie and thought Goya was a darling nickname. Their other grandmother, Grandmother Prior, called them Janine and George, and was not impressed by the oft-told tale of how Goya had come to be called that.

"When he was about two," Dr. Gavin would explain to those who inquired, "we got him a set of finger paints, and at his very first effort I said he had Goya's palette. Somehow we just got to calling him that."

"Well, I shan't," Grandmother Prior had said, and Dr. Gavin replied good-naturedly, "Suit yourself."

He was always good-humored with her, despite a truth unacknowledged by any of them—she did not like him.

"Why are you smiling?" she'd ask sharply.

"I find life amusing."

"I hope my daughter shares your sense of fun."

"She does—some of the time. I admit that I have moments of despondence myself, moments of being taken aback by life, so to speak."

"I should think so. Life is not, for some of us, all that amusing."

Yet Grandmother Prior, more than most people, had little reason to complain. Not if you considered *things* important, and she seemed to. Grandmother was what was called "comfortably off." "And that," said Dr. Gavin, a good dentist who was somehow not one of the ones who made pots of money, "is an excellent starting place for finding life agreeable." That Grandmother Prior didn't find life agreeable, that she was, on the whole, disgruntled rather than pleased about her life, past and present, and the prospects before her, seemed to be one of the things that Dr. Gavin found amusing. "Anyway, ironical," he'd say. "Irony has its funny side."

Gram, on the other hand, barely got by with the aid of Social Security and the help of her two sons. She lived with the other one, a high-school biology teacher in Michigan. On the year it was Gram's turn to spend the holidays with Jimmie's family, Grandmother Prior stayed alone in her large beautiful house in upstate Connecticut. She said she did not mind being alone, and Jimmie saw no reason to disbelieve her.

The reason they visited on alternate holidays—Christmas, Easter, a week or ten days in the summer—wasn't that the two grandmothers didn't get along with each other. It was just that they preferred not to.

Jimmie knew that if she'd had to choose between them —although she was glad enough not to have to—she'd have taken Gram.

Grandmother Prior was, in her way, okay. "My pistol granny," Jimmie had once called her, to her face.

"And what, may I ask, does that mean?"

"Oh—that you're a hotshot. A fighter," Jimmie had replied admiringly, and her grandmother had looked aloofly pleased.

Fighting every step of the way, Jimmie had thought, remembering the cosmetics on the guest-room dressing table, and the great-looking clothes hanging in the closet there. She considered it lively of Grandmother Prior to put up a battle against age. And so far, she seemed to be winning. She looked years younger than Gram.

Just the same, Gram was the one she'd take. Gram could cook and didn't call people "tomboys" and wonder aloud when they'd become "young ladies," two pretty antediluvian words in the now world of tight jeans and women's rights. But Grandmother was a paradox. With it and completely out of it. Sometimes warm, but always with this underlay of chill. Gram was just straightforwardly herself, and herself was, to Jimmie's way of thinking, just great. You could talk to her about anything. Silly things and important ones. You could even talk to her about the serious side of things that had no serious side— as her mother sometimes put it—and somehow Gram would go along. And she was fun. Like her father, Jimmie liked life, and people, to be fun.

CHAPTER THREE

"Gram!" Goya shouted, jumping up. "Lookit! We hanged a stocking up for you, too, last night, and Santa Claus filled it, too."

Gram looked toward the mantel, where one of Jimmie's socks hung, looking long and thin except at the bottom, where it bulged.

"He didn't put as much stuff in yours as in ours," Goya explained anxiously. "That's because you're so old."

"*Goya*—" Jimmie began, but Gram laughed and said Santa certainly had been clever to figure out which socks were which. "What did he leave for you?" she asked him.

Jimmie, still uneasy at prolonging this St. Nick deception, said she'd go and get the coffee started, and Gram said, "That'd be lovely, darling. I'll be right along. I thought since we were up so early, we could make poppies for breakfast. What do you say?"

Goya and Jimmie thought it would be marvelous. Gram made popovers that smelled like clouds and melted butterly in the mouth and were, in Jimmie's opinion, a version of ecstasy. As she went toward the kitchen she found herself licking her lips in a way that her mother, had she seen it, would have regarded mockingly. Her mother was almost indifferent to food. She did not like to cook, and didn't seem to care much what she ate. Jimmie had once read, or been told—she couldn't remember which—that women who don't like to cook for their families basically don't care for their families. She did not, of course, believe that.

When their parents came downstairs an hour later, the odor of popovers and bacon filled the kitchen, and Gram was stirring eggs for scrambling while Jimmie set the table in the dinette. By now she was almost frantic with hunger, although Gram seemed able to wait, and Goya was too excited by the day to notice that he hadn't eaten.

He was looking in the kaleidoscope that had come in his stocking, and observed to his father that the designs in there didn't only change shape, they changed color.

"Depends on what you're aiming at," Dr. Gavin pointed out, and Goya said he hadn't thought of that. "Did you know that, Mom?" he asked.

Mrs. Gavin, already in her chair at the table, smiled a faint pale smile and shook her head slightly.

"Have a good night, Mom?" Jimmie asked, in the jollying tone she often used with her mother.

Another faint negative with the head. "I was up for hours. Hours."

Jimmie turned away. If once, just once, her mother would say she had slept well. Even if she hadn't, even if she'd been up every single minute with her eyes wide open staring into the dark, if she'd just say *once* that she had had a good night's sleep.

Their mother was a woman who looked as if she'd gone to a good private school and then through Barnard, which she had. Still with the blonde brainy beauty of the Barnard girl, she moved through their lives—fragile, furious, and fatigued. The fragility and fatigue made her almost indifferent to housework. The fury she directed at what she called, "that troika in Washington." The White House, the Pentagon, and the Justice Department. Mrs. Gavin had a bachelor's degree in political economics, but she had never worked and was not an activist. She was not only not on the barricades, she wouldn't even hand up paving stones to those who were. In her view, there was nothing to do about the world except despise it.

"And criticize it," Dr. Gavin sometimes said. "Constantly criticize it."

"That's just a tic," she'd reply. "Ignore it."

"If it were that easy."

To Jimmie, her mother was a tense, at times terrifying, presence in a family the rest of whose members were trying to get some fun out of life.

Jimmie could not remember when her parents had gone out together, to dinner, to visit anyone, or even to a movie, in the manner of other people's parents. The effort of getting ready to do any of these things—much less actually doing them—seemed beyond Mrs. Gavin's strength. Jimmie knew kids at school whose parents ran around all the time—who gave and went to dinner parties, who got tickets for the theater or the ballet (Massic River, New Jersey, where they lived, was, after all, only half an hour from New York City), who took trips when the father had his vacation. She knew kids who went camping with their parents, and others who got sent to camps so their parents could get away together. Some of them were resentful, feeling their parents didn't pay them enough attention, and some found it just the ticket, because then they were free to do pretty much as they pleased. But nobody else she knew had a father and mother who stayed home all the time. Except for a month in the summer, when her mother took her and Goya to Grandmother Prior's to visit, her parents were home *all the time*.

Her father went to his office and came home. He did wood carving in his little study upstairs. He gardened. Being in his garden, seeing it, watching him work in it, was another version of ecstasy, on a higher plane than any food could take a person to. If he'd had more space, Jimmie knew he'd have been the best gardener in Massic River, and maybe he was the best anyway.

Her father worked and carved and gardened. Her mother read books. And periodicals and newspapers. The house was gorged with old copies of *Foreign Affairs, The Economist, Center Magazine, The New York Review of Books*. The only time her mother ever left the house was to go to the library and exchange what she'd finished for something else. If you'd asked her friends what their mothers did, Anne Ferris could've replied, "Mother teaches French at the college, and she's on the Board of the Fair Housing Commission, and she's a draft counselor, and she and Daddy go to the opera and the Philharmonic, and we have this house in Castine where she sails—" Anne could have gone on and on and on. Marcy Beggs could have said, "Mama travels and shops and plays golf and bridge." Chris Martin would simply have snorted and said, "Drinks and gets married."

But my mother reads, Jimmie thought. That was her interest, the printed word, and most of it reinforcing her conviction that the world was in ruins. She did not look at television or go to concerts or drink or shop or play golf or interest herself (except through words) in the world's affairs. She sometimes quoted E. M. Forster, "I wish neither to change the world nor corrupt it, I just wish to be left alone." And mostly, she was.

Last summer her father had suggested they drive to Maine for his vacation, maybe rent a cottage on the rockbound coast.

"Be a great change for all of us," he'd said, speaking as if there were some possibility that they'd carry through on this pipe dream. "We could eat lobster and walk on the beach and smell the pine woods. It'd be—"

"Mark, please," her mother had interrupted. "You know I'm not up to that. A cottage in Maine!" With a spurt of animation, she said, "*I* know—why don't we just stay here, making this our home base, taking little trips from here? We can go to the zoo, and the aquarium, and maybe one day take that boat that goes up the Hudson—" She'd stopped, closing her eyes. Exhausted, Jimmie had thought resentfully, at the mere inventory of all the things they might do. Making home their home base, of course.

She wasn't precisely disappointed, because she hadn't believed for a second that they'd get a cottage on the rockbound coast of Maine. But oh, how gorgeous, how glorious it would have been. She could almost smell the briny air, the piney briny air, almost see the waves crash against the rocks and fall back and foam forward again. She almost could feel herself and Goya and her father running and running down the beach, shouting—

What she'd wanted to say was, Why don't we three go,

and leave Mother here in the home base?

She had not, of course, dared.

Mrs. Gavin, in addition to being—not sickly, because aside from being tired all the time there never seemed to be anything wrong with her health—in addition, her daughter thought, to having a languishing disposition, she had a temper. Not the kind that flared. A slow-burning temper that tinged her voice and her eyes when she felt threatened, or when she was angry at the condition of the world, which she was most of the time. She loathed the Republican Administration so deeply that Jimmie sometimes wondered if she thought of anything else, and since she only had her family to talk to, it practically seemed that she thought they'd had a hand in getting it elected.

Daddy's a Democrat, and Goya and I don't vote yet, remember? Jimmie sometimes wanted to say. Her mother wouldn't vote. She despised from afar the world and all its doings. Why don't you vote, or march in peace parades, or *do* something? Jimmie wanted to say. But did not. Her mother's slow-burning anger frightened her, and she had an idea that it frightened her father, too. Goya, who had yet to develop insight into any situation or person, seemed unaware that his mother was, in effect, a quietly ticking bomb. And he didn't mind never going on trips because he knew nothing about them.

"What's the hidebound coast of Maine?" he asked Jimmie, and in spite of her frustration she'd burst out laughing.

This morning, with her yellow challis robe on, her lemon-colored hair hanging loose, Mrs. Gavin looked lovely, simply lovely. She makes the rest of us look and sound like louts, Jimmie said to herself. She and her brother were definitely Gavins—bold-featured, big-boned. Like Gram and Dad. Her mother was like some high-born creature who'd strayed down from the castle and accidentally found herself living among the plebes.

Even as she thought it, she met her mother's eyes and found a gleam of wry understanding there, as if all that went on in her mind was comprehended in that other mind. As if she were understood and forgiven for her rasping thoughts, her animosity.

Why should she forgive me? Jimmie thought. She's the one who makes everything so—so joyless around her. For *my* Christmas present, I'd have given the toboggan a miss if she'd just pull herself together. That'd be a real present, if she would just act happy. Was that too much to ask of your mother, that she act pleased with her own life part of the time, in spite of the world's wretched condition?

Apparently it was.

And yet, apparently, just now, it was not. Suddenly, in one of her swift reversals of mood, young Mrs. Gavin shed her air of languor and said, "Oh, those popovers smell ambrosial, Mother Gavin! Give me one before I swoon of yearning!"

Overdoing it, thought Jimmie, but her father, who'd been looking in Goya's kaleidoscope, brightened in a way Jimmie found touching. Gram scurried, beaming, to provide the popover.

"Coffee, Beth?" she said eagerly. "And jam. I always say, what are popovers without the jam?" Quickly she set a little place in front of her daughter-in-law and then stood back, arms folded, to enjoy the sight of Beth Gavin's pleasure in her cooking.

Jimmie herself felt a rush of grateful relief. Christmas was going to be all right, then.

"I'll put the music on," she said, and rushed off to the living room. There, for a moment, despite her hunger and even a slight greedy fear that her father might eat so many popovers that she wouldn't get as many as she wanted, she stood at the window, looking at the falling snow, already mounding on lawn and bushes. She looked at the dear little tree reflected in the cold black glass of the window, sparkling like a king's ransom in jewels. She listened to the music.

Oh, Holy night, the stars are brightly shining . . .

How beautiful it was. How really beautiful things could be, once in a while. She leaned her forehead against the cold pane and wondered why, in their house, everything had to depend on the mood of just one person.

"It isn't fair," she whispered. "Not fair, not fair."

Only Goya was unaffected. He simply went on living

in the moment, his own moment, moved only by his own reactions to it.

By mid-afternoon, except for the usual Christmas sense of getting through something that had already gone on too long (why do we get *up* so early? Jimmie asked herself, but of course she knew why), things still seemed okay. Gram was in the kitchen making the turkey dinner. Jimmie had concocted cranberry-orange relish, which she'd made each Thanksgiving and Christmas since she'd learned how in the Brownies when she was eight. She'd set the table. Her jobs, for the moment, were over.

Since, because of the snow, he couldn't use his new bike outdoors, Goya was down in the basement with it, trying to learn to balance but so far just caroming into pipes and boxes. Jimmie had stayed with him for a while, steadying the bike, but he'd decided she interfered with his progress and had dismissed her.

Her mother was upstairs lying down, asleep or going through the books and magazines that were piled on her bedside table and on the floor, and her father was in the little room across the hall from her mother's room that he called his study. He'd read *The New York Times* and was now leafing through a dental journal.

"My son-in-law, the dentist," Jimmie had heard her Grandmother Prior say one day.

"My mother, the snob," Mrs. Gavin replied, but she'd laughed a little.

Jimmie had stalked past them, her face set.

"Now see what you've done," Mrs. Gavin said. "She'll be in a mood for hours. When will you understand that you can't insult her father and get away with it?"

"Is calling him a dentist insulting him?"

"The way you say it, it is."

"Don't be silly, Beth. It's a perfectly good way to make a living. We have to have dentists."

But not marry them, that's what she means, Jimmie had thought furiously. She's a beast and a snob and Mother doesn't stand up to her. Doesn't defend Dad the way she would if— But she'd broken off there, forcing her thoughts away from her parents and their feelings for each other. She didn't actually want to know *what* they felt about each other.

All she wanted was—all she wanted—

She didn't know what she wanted, unless it was to be like other kids she knew, who were either so comfortable, or so indifferent, where their parents were concerned that they might just as well have done without them if some other arrangement, as convenient, could be made. She'd known a girl, Kate Johnstone, who'd said she'd be perfectly happy to spend all her time away at school or at camp or visiting friends. "What I want," she'd said, "is marvelous clothes and a warm house and good food, and then to be let alone. I just can't stand them nosing around in my life the way they do."

Jimmie had been appalled. "Don't you love your parents?"

Kate had laughed. "Well," she said, "if I had to choose between them, I'd opt for my mother. At least she has kicky taste in clothes and is willing to spend money. My father is stingy, and wears baggy pants, and still only has these skinny ties, and doesn't seem to mind at all that he looks like a freak. I think the least you can ask of your parents is that you be proud of their appearance. But I don't, since you ask, *love* either one of them. They aren't lovable."

Jimmie could never have been that chilly and indifferent about her relatives. She wasn't absolutely sure she loved them, except Daddy and Goya and Gram (which meant she wasn't sure about her mother and Grandmother Prior) but never ever could she have talked of them that way to someone else. But Kate wasn't the only one who said terrible things about her family to just about anyone who'd bother to listen. Jimmie knew girls who hated their parents, or said they did. Boys, in her experience, were less apt to say such things, to talk about their parents, loyally or disloyally. But then, boys, on balance, wanted to talk only about their own personalities, and could find points of interest there that were pretty obscure to an outside viewer. Strange to think that one day, probably, even Goya would be like that.

The door of her father's study was closed and she had to knock twice before there was an answer.

"Still working?" she asked when she went in.

He put aside the journal. "Not really."

"I was wondering if you wanted to go over to the park and try out my toboggan."

He looked at the clock. "Getting a bit late for that, isn't it? Your mother will be up pretty soon."

Jimmie lifted her shoulders a little at the unanswerable. She didn't meet her father's eyes, but could feel them on her.

"Tell you what—how about the three of us building a snowman?" he suggested after a pause. "There's enough snow now, I think, for a respectable snowman."

"That'd be great. I'll get Goya. Now, you dress warmly."

"Okay, Teach."

There was laughter in his tone, but she ignored it. Somebody had to care about his health, and if her mother wouldn't bother—and she wouldn't—then Jimmie would. Her mother, in fact, had such an unsolicitous attitude toward her husband and children that probably Goya, her favorite, could have gone out in the snow wearing pajamas for all she'd notice.

She, thought Jimmie, as she stumped down the cellar stairs, would make an ideal mother for Kate Johnstone.

Outside in the snow with Goya and her father, she forgot to think. She just lived in the joy of the bitter bright air, frosty with their breath, in the joy of rolling and pounding and mounding the snowman's body, the joy of the three of them, playing together.

"Goya!" she shouted, "run and get a carrot and some prunes from Gram, and your old stocking hat out of the cellarway. I'll get the head started."

She knelt and began to form a snowball with her ice-encrusted mittens while her father smoothed the snowman's body. Rolling and patting, she got her snowball to just about the proper head size.

"What do you think, Dad? This big enough?"

He came over and considered. "See if you can get about an inch more on it. This is a brainy boy we're building. Where's Goya got to, do you suppose?" He glanced toward the house, lifted his hand. "Jimmie, your mother's waving to us."

For a moment she pretended not to have heard, but

realized it would be simpler all around to look up and wave and have done with it. Then she went back, with elaborate attention, to the snow-head, but only for something to do.

Because her mother was beckoning at one or both of them. Just with a gesture, she shattered the exhilaration Jimmie had been feeling, and she heard almost without caring her father's, "Better find out what she wants. I'll be right back."

"Sure, Dad," Jimmie said, not looking up. Her father hesitated a second longer, then went toward the house. After a few steps, he stopped, turned, and said, "Jimmie —try to be a good sport."

Wiping her nose with the sleeve of her jacket, Jimmie sniffled and said, "I do try."

"I know you do," he said gently. "Well, get the head in position and I'll be out with Goya in a few minutes, okay?"

"Okay, Daddy."

When he'd gone she fumbled in her pocket for a handkerchief, blew her nose, took a deep breath, and addressed herself to the problem of getting the head affixed to the snowman's body.

Now then—she stood back, eyeing her work. The head was on lopsided, but in a way that might be effective, as if the snowman were contemplating something.

A car pulled up in front of the house and actually stopped. Jimmie looked at it curiously. They had very few visitors, and just about none that were unexpected. Probably someone wanting directions. She walked slowly to the curb.

"Can I do something for you?"

A young woman—an awfully pretty young woman with thick dark blonde hair and long mischievous eyes that sparkled—leaned out of the window, open despite the cold, and said, "Hi, are you Dr. Gavin's daughter?"

Jimmie nodded.

"Is he home?"

"Yup. He's helping us, me and my brother, build a snowman. I mean, he's in the house now, but that's what he's been doing."

"So I see. It looks a marvelous snowman. I love making them."

She got out of the car and sauntered across the lawn, Jimmie following. She wore tight scarlet ski pants, short boots, and a white wool jacket. Her hair swirled a little as she walked.

What the heck, Jimmie said to herself. "Who are you?" she blurted. Realizing how abrupt that sounded, she said hastily, "That is, hello and all. I was just wondering—"

"I'm Emily Copeland."

That's supposed to mean something to me? "I'm Jimmie—I mean, Janine Gavin."

"Which do you prefer? Which should I call you?"

Why should you call me anything? Jimmie thought.

"Hasn't your father mentioned me?" said the young woman. She reached up and tapped the snowman on the head. "I like the way he's tipping the noggin. Gives him a moody look. Aren't you going to give him a face?"

"No. I mean, yes we're going to give him a face. But no, my father hasn't mentioned you. Should he have?"

"I'm his new assistant."

"Assistant? *Dental* assistant? You?"

The girl laughed. "I don't know whether to take that as a compliment or not."

Take it any way you want, Jimmie thought. She felt an overwhelming wariness about this—person, this Emily Copeland.

"Where's Miss Kavanagh?"

Miss Kavanagh had been Dad's assistant forever and she looked, in no *way*, like this. She looked—well, like Miss Kavanagh, who'd been somebody's dental assistant forever.

"She's retired. I can't understand why your father didn't say anything."

"Well, I guess probably he did. He probably told my mother, all right. Maybe he even did mention you, only I didn't pay attention."

Except that she would have paid attention and he had not told them of Miss Kavanagh's retirement, and it was peculiar.

Dr. Gavin, coming out of the house with Goya and the

trimmings for the snowman, stopped on seeing Miss Copeland. "Hey, hello. What brings you here?"

"Nothing, really. Just passing by and saw your house and thought I'd introduce myself. Janine—Jimmie—has been entertaining me."

Maybe so, thought Jimmie, but it wasn't my intention.

"I didn't know Miss Kavanagh was retiring," she said sharply to her father. "You didn't say anything about it, did you?"

"I didn't know myself until a couple of weeks ago. It was sort of a sudden decision. She's going to Florida with her sister—you remember her sister—well, they inherited their parents' house down there. Just in time, as Miss Kavanagh says, for her and her sister to retire into it. So that's what they're doing. I was lucky she found Miss Copeland for me."

"Yes, weren't you."

"Say, come along and help us with this snowman here," said Dr. Gavin. "Oh, this is my son, Goya. Goya, this is Miss Copeland."

"What a wonderful name. How are you, Goya?"

"Better."

"Oh? Have you been sick?"

"He always says that," Dr. Gavin explained. "We haven't figured out why yet, have we, Jimmie?"

"Nope."

"I've never heard of anyone named Goya, except Goya, before," said Miss Copeland, smiling. Her teeth, Jimmie thought, should double a dentist's practice overnight.

"Well, actually his name is George. You see, when he was about two we got him a set of—"

The tall youngish man and the tall young woman walked off, with Goya, carefully carrying a carrot and two prunes and his old stocking cap, between them.

Jimmie stood looking after them, then glanced up at a bedroom window where her mother stood, holding back the curtains with one hand, the fingers of the other hand laid across her lips in a gesture of—surprise, was it? Suddenly she noticed her daughter watching her, and gave a little wave and a smile before she disappeared into the room behind her.

CHAPTER FOUR

The night before the Christmas holidays ended, Jimmie dreamed about the school bus. In her dream it was bigger and yellower than in real life (when it was big and yellow enough) and it tended to bulge and buckle and speed off the edges of cliffs. In life or a dream, the school bus was a roaring rolling prison in which people were trapped morning and afternoon.

Jimmie, who boarded early in the run, usually was able to sit up front, close to the driver, a man everybody called Bunny because of his ears. She sort of wished she knew his real name, but after riding with him for months it seemed impolitely late to ask. Bunny was supposed to keep his eye on things, but seemed to have all he could do to keep on the road, and Jimmie often wondered how anyone could drive with fifty-four kids of different ages shoving and yelling behind him like a lot of wild animals. Sitting at the front of the bus didn't help, because Bunny was no protection. He occupied himself, fiercely, with driving, never glancing in his mirror to see what went on behind. Sometimes Jimmie told herself that they could pull into the school yard with ten bodies back there and old Bunny would be the most surprised of all.

At the corner this morning Anne Ferris, among others, was already waiting. She had on a new jacket—navy blue, lined with something white and fleecy. She wore blue and red striped tights, a blue mini, black boots, and white

earmuffs. With her dark hair and blazing blue eyes, she
was stunningly pretty. Jimmie, who was pretty herself, felt
less so in the presence of Anne. She thought it had something to do with clothes. While she fully expected to work
up an interest one day in the matter of what she had on,
so far all she asked was that it be old and reasonably
clean. Of course, Anne's mother liked clothes, and liked
to go shopping with her. That might make a difference.

"Jimmie! Did you have a good holiday?"

"Just fine. How was Maine?"

"Dandy. But I'm glad we're back. Why are people usually glad when vacations are over?"

"I guess because they—I mean we—get bored so easily.
My father says that Americans are trapped in the Puritan
work ethic, which held that work is man's salvation.
That's what he says, anyway."

"Oh, I don't like to work," Anne said. "I just get tired
of everybody else not working."

The bus pulled up and Bunny shoved the door open
with a long lever. He grunted what could be taken for a
greeting as they got on. Most of the boarding students
mumbled something back or ignored him, but Anne
smiled radiantly and said, "Bunny! Here you are! Did you
have a marvy Christmas?"

"You know what the best part was," he said, but a
smile cracked his stone face slightly.

"But of course. Only honestly, didn't you miss us one
teeny bit?"

Already some sort of scrap was in progress at the back
of the bus and Bunny, yanking the gear into first, re-
verted to his customary sourness. "Not so's you'd notice,"
he said.

Just the same, Anne could always bring a smile, however brief, to a masculine face. Her effect on females was
something otherwise. Jimmie had noticed how even senior
girls tended to look at her appraisingly, knowing she was
already a threat to them. Probably, Jimmie thought, all
her life Anne will be regarded by other women as a
threat. Some girls just were like that.

Emily Copeland, now. Was she the kind that just by
existing made other women insecure? She'd frolicked in

the snow with them that day, giving every appearance of being an open-air good-sport sort, everything jolly and straight from the shoulder. Not an ounce of coquetry in her, you'd have said, to look at her, to listen to her. Just the beautiful dental assistant playing with the boss's family, and the boss, in the snow. Not a sidelong glance, not a flirtatious gesture. So why had Jimmie felt vibrations in the cold air that finally drove her into the house, leaving her father, her brother, and Miss Copeland to finish the snowman she no longer cared about and had avoided looking at ever since?

Miss Copeland had not come around again, and had not been mentioned, in Jimmie's presence anyway, since that afternoon. In fact, she'd almost forgotten that her father had a new assistant until now, looking at Anne, she recalled that other female face, flushed with cold and laughing.

"What's up?" Anne asked. She burrowed in her large purse, produced a mirror and studied her appearance carefully. After a moment, with evident satisfaction, she tucked the mirror back in place. "Thought I had a smudge or something, the way you were looking at me. Oh, murder—let's get under the seats, Jimmie. Here come the gum chewers."

Bunny drew up at a corner where a group of high-school jocks was assembled, pushing one another around and shouting and now and again pretending to dance. Seeing them, you might just have enjoyed their high spirits, if they hadn't, every one, been chewing gum. Tiny pale pink bladders erupted from their mouths and burst in the cold air before achieving any size.

Bunny shoved the door open, almost snarling, and they piled in noisily, shouting obscenities, ramming their way toward the rear of the bus. They were like a victorious army, boisterous and overbearing, and they took up their positions like an army ready for fresh blood. Looked at in one way, their weapons were harmless enough. No switch blades, no rocks in the fist. Something subtle, Jimmie thought, as befits their middle-class class. What they aimed at their victims was bubble gum. They sent the clotted pellets sailing the length of the bus, not seeming to aim but often hitting a mark.

Anne sighed and took a plastic head-scarf from her bag, tying it under her chin as she slid down in the seat. Jimmie, sliding with her, until, it was to be hoped, the tops of their heads were protected, wished she'd ever remember to provide herself with a plastic defense. The difficulty being that this gang of hoods had different ploys, and you couldn't come prepared for everything. Sometimes they rolled acorns or marbles down the aisles, and once a boy had actually slipped on one and broken his arm. Nothing in the way of reprisal had occurred, since Bunny disclaimed any knowledge of the accident except to say that he had not been braking suddenly or going over a bump too fast or in any way driving his vehicle in a manner to endanger his precious cargo.

"Kid just musta took a spill," Bunny had said stoutly to the principal, in the hearing of all his passengers. And no one had contradicted him, not even the boy with the broken arm.

"No telling," Anne had said to Jimmie later, *"what* those Cro-Magnons would think of in the way of getting back at you."

This morning, however, they subsided faster than usual, and Jimmie and Anne were too relieved to wonder why. Cautiously they straightened in their seats and, not looking around, waited for signs of renewed activity from the rear.

"Wonder what they're cooking up now?" Anne whispered. "They are *too* quiet. Oh,. well, thanks for little blessings. What did you get for Christmas? *I* got this luscious jacket and a pants suit you'll never *believe,* it's so yummy—raspberry bells and a jerkin and this white ruffled shirt. It's for in the spring. And a couple of sweaters, and, my dear, some Miss Dior—at forty dollars an *ounce,* mind."

"Who got you that?"

"My father, who else? Half an ounce. Mother got a whole ounce of *Joy.* And he gave her a medallion, gold with a sapphire on it. It says on it, 'More than yesterday, less than tomorrow.' Isn't that darling? Mother gave me *Jane Eyre,* have you ever read it? I wonder if Charlotte Brontë ever actually *knew* a man like Mr. Rochester. He's enough to ruin a girl for real live men forever. Have you read it?"

Jimmie preferred books by Loren Eiseley, Josephine Johnson, Konrad Lorenz, writers like that, but she wouldn't say to Anne that love stories just did not interest her. Surely at a time not too far away they would, because Women's Lib or no Women's Lib, girls had to care about love and men like Mr. Rochester.

("Manumission for women," her mother had said, "will never be complete, because the majority of them will insist upon having a yoke put on them by some man— thereby, of course, putting one on his shoulders, too."

"What's manumission?" Jimmie had asked, and her mother had said, "Oh, Jimmie—really.")

But as to romance, in which she still had no interest, she vaguely supposed that it would coincide with the time when she began to have periods. Anne had been menstruating for two years and was mysterious and proud and a bit complacent about it, as if it were not something that had happened to her, but something she'd achieved. When she had a note from home excusing her from gym, she'd say to Jimmie, "My period, you know," rather in the way of a club member speaking to someone who unaccountably hadn't got in.

Jimmie was fourteen, and not a sign yet. In desperation she'd suggested to her mother that there must be something wrong with her and they'd gone to the doctor who said her case was not unusual and to come back in six months if she hadn't started yet. She hadn't discussed it with her mother again and mostly managed not to think about it, but somewhere in the reaches of her mind she was always aware that in this, as in some other ways, she was not like other girls. Bright enough, of course—Anne said she could get A's just by looking out the window— but backward, just the same. Arrested.

A shout went up from the rear of the bus. "Hey, Bunny Rabbit! Pull over. Guy back here's gonna puke!"

With a muttered oath, Bunny slid to the side of the road, thrust open the door and said, "Whoever it is, get him down and outa here, pronto!"

"Sure. Sure thing, Bunny. *Here* we go, fella—"

Four or five boys jammed their way down the crowded aisle, trampling books and feet and gym bags. The boy in front was holding his stomach and moaning. "Help me down, willya, Bunny?" he said, pretending to retch.

Anne, Jimmie noticed, had covered her eyes with her hands and was pushing her fingers against the fluffy ear-muffs. Here nothing, see nothing, thought Jimmie. How right she is. Jimmie did what she could to escape, squeezing her eyes shut, sticking her fingers in her ears so hard that her head rang.

Bunny, with another oath, this time quite audible, got down on the sidewalk and held up his hand to assist the sufferer, who immediately straightened and, with a bellow of laughter, shoved the lever of the door shut, which locked the at first dumbfounded and then maniacally en-raged driver out in the cold. The five big—awfully big, thought Jimmie, opening her eyes and dropping her hands to her lap in confusion and even some fright—the five huge boys beat one another on the back and screamed with amusement, sending their exultant glances around the bus as if expecting all passengers to be gladdened.

"They're crazy," Anne whispered. "Starkers. Oh, my God. You don't think they're going to *hi*jack us, do you?"

"Hush," Jimmie whispered back. Her voice shook, even on the one word, and she dared not say more. But what would they do, these—these lunatics?

So far, they were only laughing so loud and congratu-lating one another to such a preoccupied extent that they didn't pay attention to Bunny, who'd gone around to the back exit door, opened it from the outside, and crawled in.

"Okay!" he bellowed. "Okay, you buncha goons! Get back in your seats and don't let me hear a peep outa any of ya. Not one more squeak, got it?"

"You don't want us to peep, Bunny? Ah, gee whiz. We're just not peepless types, you know?"

"Full of peep, we are," said the ersatz invalid, making the word slyly suggestive.

"Well, you just better hold them peeps this morning," Bunny said, sounding all at once menacing as, shoving and elbowing, he made his way to the front. "Get outa my way!" He pushed one of his tormentors so hard that the boy fell across Jimmie and Anne. He looked down briefly, blinked at Anne and said, "Hmm, what have we *here?"*

Jimmie could feel Anne trembling, could almost feel her heart pounding. Her own stomach was in knots, but she sat frozenly still, as the warm repulsive bulk pressed against her shoulder.

"All right," said Bunny. *"Okay.* That does it. We're going straight to the cops. I've put up with you creeps for months, but I'm damned if I'll put up with any more."

The boy straightened, looked at Bunny, then at his friends. "Think he means it?"

"You better believe I mean it. I'm going to prefer charges against the bunch of you." He lifted his voice. "That goes for you back there, too, and don't think I don't know who you are, either, and don't think I'm scared of you, you bunch of—"

"Hey, hey," said the recovered patient, who appeared to be a leader of sorts, "you got us all wrong, Bunny Boy. We were just having a little fun. High spirits, you know."

"High spirits!" Bunny put the bus in gear and started off, fast for a school bus. "High on something all right. I betcha somebody's gonna get arrested for possession, that's what I bet."

"Hey, for Chr— I mean, for Pete's sake, fella. Don't take us to the fuzz. We'll be late for school, our very first morning."

Jimmie couldn't help a snicker escaping, which earned her an approving glance from the leader, a glance she didn't relish. Still, it had been an awfully funny thing to say. Provided it hadn't been just plain dumb. With this bunch you couldn't tell.

Bunny, leaving them in suspense for a while, drove with his eyes front, apparently now pretending that he was all alone in the bus, or driving a load of cattle, and there was no point in reasoning with cattle, was there?

In a few blocks it became clear that they were, after all, heading for the high school, as the route prescribed. But something about their driver now, something about the set of his shoulders and the mean look in his eye when he pulled up at the school door, kept even that rowdy gang subdued.

One of them, as they stepped down, said, "Hey, you aren't really gonna fink on us, are you?"

"You just stew about it, fella. I got a bus full of witnesses, and I got plans for you guys, believe me. Just keep it in mind."

"We'll have to tell the principal," said a bossy girl named Faith Powers. "We must all go in a body and complain."

"You go in a body and complain," Jimmie muttered, walking off. She found Anne beside her, and they proceeded in silence to their lockers.

"Do you suppose they're going to the principal?" Anne asked, putting away her jacket and earmuffs and then, in front of her locker mirror, combing her dark hair with positively mermaidy gestures. She touched an index finger to her tongue and smoothed her brows.

"I don't know, and I don't care," Jimmie said. "I've had so many nightmares about that bus that I want to tell you this morning was like a dream come true."

Anne giggled, then patted her hand. "Well, it's all over until this afternoon. Put it from your mind."

"Fat chance."

Still, there was nothing else to do, so she got on with trying to forget about the ride home, and sometime during the morning had the inspiration to telephone her father, who got out of his office about the same time that she and Anne got out of school, and ask for a ride home.

Dr. Gavin picked them up at the school gate and did not, as he ordinarily would have, ask why he'd been pressed into service in this manner. Usually he was curious about everything. Today he greeted them pleasantly, and drove in silence.

"How's your new assistant doing?" Jimmie asked suddenly.

"Huh? Who? Oh, Miss Copeland, you mean. Oh, she's fine, fine. Working out very well."

Jimmie, desperate in several directions, tried to read indifference into his voice, but what she seemed to hear was a man trying to sound indifferent. Or was that just a smallminded figment? When he went on to tell them a particularly funny story about a patient of his who wanted Novocain just while having his teeth cleaned, she relaxed and was even able to rebuke herself for what she'd been —imagining. This was her *father*—not a masher who got flirted with by the beauteous dental assistant and then went off hand in hand with her into the sunset or to South America, like in a crummy movie.

This was her *father*.

CHAPTER FIVE

At breakfast the next morning Jimmie said, "Daddy, you wouldn't want to get to the office early this morning, I suppose?"

"You suppose right. I wouldn't."

Jimmie nodded, nibbled an English muffin, and wondered if Gram or her father would be the first to say, "Why?" They were inquisitive, and would not be able to leave such a request uninvestigated.

"Hand me the jam, will you, Goya?" she asked. "Thanks."

"Why?" said Gram.

"Why what?"

"Why did you ask your father if he wanted to get to the office early?"

"Oh. Well, I thought if he did want to, for some reason, he could drive Anne and me to school."

"Why should I have some special reason this morning?" Dr. Gavin asked, sharply, for him.

Jimmie's mind made the transition from the bus to Miss Copeland. Firmly she reminded herself that anything she was thinking about Miss Copeland was not only in her own head alone, it was also unworthy and shoddy and—

"For the matter of that," her father went on, "why did you ask me to drive you and Anne home yesterday? The only other time I remember doing it was when the school bus broke down that time."

"It may be breaking down again," Jimmie said grimly. "I mean, passengerwise and busdriverwise."

Dr. Gavin laughed.

"What do you mean?" Gram persisted.

Jimmie looked at her father, her grandmother, her little brother, all of them in this cozy little dinette off the kitchen where the morning sun was flooding in, making a row of geraniums on the windowsill flame with color, and wished she could just stay here with them, warm and safe. The thought of the bitter cold outside, the cold and alarming bus ride ahead, lay stonily across her spirits.

She told them about yesterday morning's ride. Goya listened as if it were another adventure of the Round Table, but her grandmother was horrified.

"You mean nobody does anything about these roughnecks?"

"Not really. There was a girl one time who got a wad of chewing gum in her hair, and by the time we got to school she was hysterical, trying to pull it out and it was all tangled up and the school nurse took her home. They had to cut off lots of her hair, too. But she said she didn't know who'd done it. Come to that, she didn't. I mean, they just all gang up back there and who's to know which one's doing what? I mean, I don't dare even look *back*. I don't want to catch anybody's eye. That girl, Kate Johnstone, the one who got her hair cut, she goes to private school now. She wouldn't come back to our school." She glanced at her father, who hadn't said anything yet. "I sure wish Mother could drive a car," she muttered.

("Your mother can't drive a car?" a girl at school had said to her one day. "But how in the world does she get around?"

"She doesn't. She doesn't want to get around, except to the library and she can walk to that."

"But—how do *you* get around?"

"Bike. Bus. Sometimes my father drives us somewhere."

"How do you get your groceries, for Pete's sake?"

"They're delivered."

"But this is crazy. How does your mother get her clothes?"

"Sends for them from the newspaper, or department-store catalogs," Jimmie said uncomfortably, wishing she hadn't got into this quiz.

"Well. Well, I never *heard* of such a thing." The girl had sounded admiring. "I thought every human being over the age of sixteen knew how to drive a car. Fancy not being able to. Your mother must be sort of *in*-teresting."

"Yeah. She is.")

And still her father hadn't said anything.

"I'm not making it up, if that's what you mean," she said hotly.

"I didn't say you were making it up. Exaggerating, possibly?"

"Possibly. Not much."

"Perhaps I'd better go and see your principal."

"Oh, Daddy—that wouldn't do any good at all. A man who can't even get the kids to quit chewing gum in class won't stop them from pitching it around the bus. You'd only get me in trouble."

"When I went to school," Gram said, "we weren't allowed to chew gum. Nasty dirty habit, and very bad for the teeth."

"Actually, that's not so," said Dr. Gavin. "If it's sugarless, it's beneficial to the teeth. Gives the gums exercise and cleans the teeth. But I hate the way it looks, myself. Chop, chop, chop—" He moved his mouth around noisily, pretending to have a wad of spearmint in there.

Jimmie jumped to her feet. "What's the matter with you?" she shouted. "Here I am telling you something awfully important, *and* awful, and you're talking about the goddarn therapeutic effect of gum-chewing!"

"Sit down, Jimmie."

She hesitated, then slumped to her seat.

"I'm sorry," her father said. "I guess I was trying to divert you. Or make the whole thing less—less looming."

"How less or more something looms depends on who it's being loomed over."

"Well, then—what do you want me to do? If it really is as bad as you say, every day in every way, and you won't let me go to your principal, then yes—I'll leave early for the office every morning and drive you and

Anne to school, and I'll come around every afternoon and pick you up."

"You make it sound so stupid. You make me sound stupid and childish and whiny. And it isn't fair."

"I'm trying to figure out something that is fair. But I can't help realizing that practically a townful of kids ride those buses every day. They can't all get their parents to drive them."

"Okay," Jimmie said, defeated. "You're right." She got up again, took her books from under the table. "I have to be going. 'Bye, everybody."

She went into the hall and pulled on her pea jacket, first jamming her arm in the torn lining of one of the sleeves. As she was struggling to untangle herself, she sensed her father behind her. Turning briefly, she leaned against his chest and he put his arms around her.

"Don't worry about me," she said with a sigh. "I'm fine."

He hugged her, released her, and tipped her chin up with his tapering fingers. "Sure you're fine," he said, dropping a kiss on her brow. "Why don't you sew that lining up, or get my mother to?"

As she walked toward the bus stop, Jimmie blinked back tears. It was strange, in life, how moments of such sweetness came that you almost couldn't bear them.

The snow of Christmas had long since hardened into dirty walls along the curbs and patches of stale-colored ice on the streets. The sky was hard and gray as a sidewalk. People walked in a winter attitude, eyes down for fear of falling. Jimmie had noticed before how in the spring people lifted their chins and looked ahead, or even upward.

"Hi," said Anne, ahead of her as usual. "What jollies do you suppose we'll be treated to this morning?"

Jimmie didn't answer.

After a while, she said, "It's late. Do you suppose they've murdered Bunny?"

"Or he's finally killed one of them. Preferably all." When the bus arrived, ten minutes late, they stared in astonishment at the driver. Not Bunny. A new one. A young one, with long hair, an Indian band around his forehead, a big fleece-lined jacket torn at the elbows, and heavy laced boots.

He smiled as they got on, and Anne said softly, on a long shaky sigh, "Oh-my-*word* . . . will you just look at that."

"Name's Dick Mosher," the new driver said. "Other fellow had a heart attack last night. From what I hear of this run, it's no wonder."

As they settled into their usual seats, Anne gripped Jimmie's arm. "Do you be*lieve* it? I mean, look at him! He must be the most gorgeous thing since—since—" She was speechless.

"Since Mr. Rochester?"

"Oh, yes," Anne breathed. "He must be just like Mr. Rochester when he was young. When Mr. Rochester was young, I mean—"

Absolutely babbling, Jimmie thought.

"How old is he, do you suppose?" Anne whispered.

"Forty."

"Oh, Jimmie." Anne giggled. "No, really—how old, do you think?"

"He's too old for you, and there's no think about it."

Anne didn't seem to hear. She was devouring the driver with her eyes, though when he glanced in his rearview mirror and caught her at it, she turned in confusion to the window, then to Jimmie. Her cheeks were noticeably flushed.

Jimmie, figuring that Dick Mosher was probably used to having this effect on girls, felt sorry for Anne. And for the first time in our acquaintance, too, she thought.

"Here comes the gum squad," she pointed out.

"Who cares?" But Anne got out her plastic scarf and Jimmie realized that again she'd forgotten to provide herself with one.

"Here," said Anne, thrusting at Jimmie a transparent scarf like her own. "I brought it for you, because you're too forgetful to get one for yourself."

"Gee, thanks," said Jimmie, touched. She tied it under her chin as the huskies piled on board.

They yelped at the sight of Dick.

"Hey, man, lookit this, willya?"

"What have we got here? A red injun?"

"Where's old Bunny Rabbit, huh? Where is *he?*"

They did not make their way, as was customary, to the rear of the bus, but hung around forward, seeming almost to ring the new driver, who told them his name was Dick Mosher and to sit down, please.

They sat, a few on each other's laps, since there were not enough seats forward.

"Say, your hair's too sweet, Dicky. What's your secret? Curlers? Or is that a natural wave?" said the leader.

"What I like," one of his minions offered, "is the Hopi headdress. Hope it's Hopi, anyhow. Maybe for treats he'll wear his feathers one day, hey?"

Dick snorted and kept driving.

The leader, looking around restlessly, spied a boy behind him, a boy from Jimmie's freshman class, named Artie. He was short and shy. He had on an obviously hand-knitted stocking cap, which the leader snatched from his head.

"Here's a little fellow in his Christmas togs. Doesn't he look a treat? Some of you cats get back there," he directed, and sent the hat, which he'd rolled in a ball, sailing up the aisle.

"Hey, hey. Good catch!" he shouted. "Skim it back, willya? We'll make like it's summertime and we're on the beach, playing with our rubber ball."

"Hey, gimme my cap," Artie said stoutly, standing up. "My mother knitted that. You give it back!"

"Ah, but you'll spoil our fun," the leader said. "You'll—"

"Give'm back his cap," Dick directed, braking gently for a car ahead, then picking up speed again.

"What? Whatcha say, Dickie? Can't hear over all this racket. Awful, the way people behave on this bus. A downright disgrace."

Artie's cap was sailing back and forth, and he was making futile attempts to snare it.

"I said—give the kid back his cap."

The leader shook his head hopelessly. "Not an effing word can I hear, old buddie. There's this noise pollution problem—"

The new driver pulled the bus to the side of the road and a surprised silence fell among the passengers as he turned to face them.

"Well, now you can hear me. Hand the kid back his cap, is what I said."

"Oh, *that's* what you said." The leader considered. "And if we don't?"

"I'll knock your heads together." Dick smiled. He had a pleasant, easy smile and seemed to be about six foot four.

"Oh, now. You couldn't do that," the leader pointed out. "I mean, man, you'd lose your job the minute we got to the old institution of lower learning, as we like to call the institution of lower learning we go to. Yup, sure enough, that'd be what'd happen."

Dick reached over and took the leader by the arm. "Only if someone told on me." He gazed at his busload calmly. "Don't imagine anyone would."

"Son, you don't *know* us. We're natural-born squealers, aren't we, guys?" He appealed to his gang, but they, for once, did not seem to stand solidly behind him. They shrugged, and didn't laugh, and looked away.

They already sort of like Dick, Jimmie thought. He's calm and has a soft voice and a great smile. And, of course, the muscle. Everybody likes muscle.

"Now, let's have your attention," Dick was saying. "I'll make it quick. I plan not to get a heart attack and suggest nobody tries to give me one. I want everything to be nice and pleasant on this run from now on, and figure to see it goes the way I want it. Now, you—" he said to the leader, "are going to give the fellow back his cap, *now*. And then you're going to sit here just behind me and tell me how to get to this school of yours."

The leader gaped. "You mean you don't know where it is?"

"How should I know where it is? I didn't go to it, and I've never driven a bus before. So—" He smiled again. "You all have the privilege of being with me on the very first day of a job I can see is going to offer challenges." He looked at the leader. "Sit down and start navigating. And if," Dick said, lifting his voice and looking down the rows of seats, "he tries any funny stuff like sending me up a one-way street the wrong way or directing me to the town dump, you people straighten him out. Got it?"

There was a roar of agreement from a bewitched bus-load of students and Dick settled down to drive under the accurate directions of the erstwhile leader, who seemed as fascinated as anyone by the new driver.

"Well—my goodness," Jimmie said. She was going to go on to say how the strong-arm stuff always prevailed, even when it came elegantly packaged, as in this case. Just another version of the good guy with the fastest gun, she'd been about to say, but decided she'd sound too much like her mother.

She turned to Anne, who was looking pretty tragic, even in profile. "What's the matter with you?"

"Oh, Jimmie . . . I've fallen in love."

"That fast?"

"That's how it happens," Anne said, from her position of superior knowledge. She put a hand to her forehead in a gesture that Jimmie thought should have looked silly, but somehow did not.

"You feel okay?"

"I feel glorious, and miserable. I have a feeling that I am going to suffer horribly."

Jimmie shook her head irritably. But she could not, looking at Dick, extend her irritation to him.

As they got off the bus in the school yard, Anne stopped Dick and said, "How *is* Bunny?" and Jimmie realized, with a start of self-reproach, that none of them had really reacted to poor Bunny's plight at all. Even Anne might well be asking about him less to find out how the old bus driver was than simply to talk to the new one.

We're awful, Jimmie thought, determining, when Dick said that Bunny was going to be in the hospital for quite a while, to go and see him there.

But she never did.

CHAPTER SIX

It was the middle of January, and Gram, whose visit was to end the following day, was in her room trying to finish up Dr. Gavin's shirts. She was turning collars and sewing on buttons. Jimmie thought it was pretty nice of Gram to fix it so Dad could put on the first shirt he picked out of the drawer. She knew that some mornings he had to put aside three or four before finding one with enough buttons on to make it wearable. And lots of his collars were frayed, but he wouldn't buy new ones because he was aware, from boyhood memories, that it was perfectly possible to turn them and so make the shirt do for several more months. Dr. Gavin was not a man to throw his money about.

He did not, for instance, see why a woman should wear perfume or use bath oil. "Although, if you really *want* them," he'd said to his wife. But that had been in the far past, and except for a present from her mother now and then, Mrs. Gavin went unscented and said it didn't matter to her in the least. Dr. Gavin believed her and Jimmie did not.

Gram had also seen to Goya's clothes, had repaired the lining of Jimmie's pea jacket and let down several skirts for her, since skirts were getting longer and Jimmie had no notion of how to let down and face a hem.

"Marcy Beggs just gets all new things," she said now to Gram, who smiled but didn't reply, as if such a state of things defied comment. Gram didn't toss money about, either. She and Dad believed that thrift was a virtue not to be confused with stinginess. In their case, Mrs. Gavin sometimes said, there tended to be some overlapping.

Jimmie and her grandmother were together in Gram's room—the guest room—peacefully conversing. Goya was next door with his friend and foe, Kenny. Mrs. Gavin was in her room with the door closed. Jimmie was content to be here, listening to the tiny heartbeat of Gram's traveling clock, watching her grandmother's swift competent hands at work. Why, she wondered idly, does Gram look so much older than Grandmother Prior does, in one way, and at the same time younger? Gram had lots more wrinkles, and her hands had these knobby knuckles that Dad said came from arthritis, and she certainly was a dowdy dresser. But, just the same—

Well, she knew what it was, but out of an almost reluctant loyalty to Grandmother Prior, hadn't exactly phrased it to herself before. It was simple. Gram had a pleasant expression and Grandmother did not.

"Why do you usually look as if you thought something nice might happen? Or already was happening?"

Gram snipped a thread with the little gold scissors Mrs. Gavin had given her for Christmas. She considered for a moment, a habit both she and her son had, of not giving you the answer before you'd finished asking the question. Jimmie loved that in them.

"Perhaps because I've been fortunate all my life. So much so, that I sometimes feel a little guilty. I had parents I loved, who loved me. A husband who has been taken from me but is *with* me," she said with calm confidence, putting a hand over her heart to show where her husband still lived. "My sons are wonderful people, who still care for me. So many people I know seem to lose their children, once they're grown. And then," she added, "I have my utterly lovely grandchildren. What in the world more could a woman want?"

"Women want a lot more, these days," Jimmie pointed out.

"You mean the Women's Liberation Movement? Oh

well, that's another thing, and of course in many ways I approve of what they stand for. Almost all ways. They're shrill and silly at times, and make themselves a spectacle, so that people are distracted from realizing the very real good sense and fairness of what they are fighting for. I had an aunt, Aunt Cora, who was a Suffragette. They were vilified, too, you know. Spat on by policemen, laughed at by men. But they had a goal and were willing to endure such things to achieve it."

"I've read about them. I think they were *very* impressive."

Gram looked briefly surprised. "I keep forgetting how much older young people are today than they were when I was young. At fourteen I think I was still going to bed at eight and reading *Little Women*. Loving it, too. *Little Women*, I mean. Do girls still read that?"

"Some do. I read it, but ages ago."

"Did you love it?"

"I liked it. Some of it. I liked Jo, all right, but she was sort of a nineteenth-century Women's Lib type, wasn't she? Anyway, Louisa May Alcott was. The others, in the book, they're too much. Actually *pleased* to be subservient. I mean, really, Gram—that Amy calling Laurie, 'My lord.' Too antediluvian."

Gram laughed a little, as if pleased. "It's so interesting to have a granddaughter like you. Are all your friends concerned with Women's Liberation?"

"Nope. I'm not really all that interested myself, yet. I mean, I expect I will be, some time. I expect lots of things will be important to me that aren't just yet. Fourteen is such a nothing time, you know? Just sort of marking time, waiting to be grown up. I mean—" She lowered her voice, then consciously elevated it again, "Gram, do you realize that I haven't even got my period yet?"

Her grandmother blinked a little, as if taken aback, but quickly recovered. Jimmie could almost hear her telling herself how young people were so much more outspoken these days than they'd been when *she* was a girl. And how that was a good thing. Gram was a sport.

"I suppose fourteen is a bit late," she said thoughtfully. "Have you asked the doctor?"

"*He* took it calmly enough. Told me to come back in six months if nothing happens. That was a month ago."

"I—suppose your mother has prepared you?" Gram asked so delicately that Jimmie hid a smile.

"Well, you know Mother. She's quite prepared to discuss the history of the Socialist Party with me, or explain how Congress works. Or doesn't work, more likely. But she's not panting to discuss my personal problems with me. I think she really would figure they were too personal."

"This might—not that it is yet—but it might be a health problem," old Mrs. Gavin said, frowning.

"I expect if it actually becomes one, Mother'll do something about it. And I've read the books. It's not all that unusual. Just unusual enough to annoy me. But the books really lay it out for you."

"And you read whenever you want to know about something, don't you?"

"It's a way to find out about stuff. What it is about books, is—well, here you are, this one single person, having this one single life and if you didn't read it'd all be pretty limited, wouldn't it? Anyway, that's what I think; of course, it doesn't always work. I tried some books on Women's Liberation, but most of them bored me. I gave Mother Kate Millet's book for her birthday. Not that she ever *does* anything, but she thinks that way. Only when I asked her about the Women's Lib, she said it had come too late to help her, and then wouldn't tell me what she meant."

Gram was folding the shirts, putting away her sewing things. "I suspect she meant that the liberation movement can't alter the training that women of her generation, and certainly older women, received. We were taught by society, by men, and by our *mothers*, mind you, that our role was to serve, and that our goal was marriage. Your mother is a young woman, comparatively speaking, of course, but nearly every woman her age felt literally disgraced, a *failure*, if she did not succeed in marrying somebody. In some cases, practically anybody, just to be married. Even a woman as well-educated and *prepared* to be on her own as your mother. They just had to get married. I breathe a sigh of relief when I see that somehow girls today have a greater sense of their own worth than to feel it must be demonstrated by some man's signature on a contract."

"Gram, you are the greatest. No, I mean it. You're tops. I'll tell you something funny, while we're on the subject of grandmothers, I think Grandmother Prior is really more with it in some ways than Mom. Of course, in a way Grandmother Prior just hates men, because of what Grandfather did—but whatever the reason, it comes out to she goes along with new ideas quicker than my mother does. Ideas about the importance of being married, I mean."

"You really have been reading," Gram said. "Why are you laughing? What did I say that was funny?"

"Oh—I don't know if I can explain. Well, okay—you think that if a girl works something out in her head, for herself, then she's been reading. Probably some book by a man, at that. I mean, I can't have figured that out about Grandmother Prior for myself, because I'm a girl or too young or something. Do you see?"

"I see," Gram said ruefully. "I should be chastened."

"No, you shouldn't. Not ever. You really are just about my best person to talk with, besides Anne. I love talking with Daddy but not about—well, there are things you don't discuss with a man. And when I asked *him* about Women's Lib, he said he believed in equal pay for equal work, and he said in that sort of pompous way he gets sometimes, 'I'd vote for a woman for President, *if* she were qualified.' He sounded *so* pleased with himself for saying that, but also as if he knew darn well a woman would never be qualified. *He* says a woman by nature is devious and wants to be. He says women prefer to get what they want by pampering and wheedling and—I forget what else. Masculine huffing and puffing, if you ask me."

"But there are a great many women like that."

"Sure. Maybe most. But that's because they've been forced over the centuries to *be* devious. And that forces them to be practically schizophrenic. My friend Anne Ferris is actually a brainy and original type, and if she's just with girls, it shows. But put her around a boy! She sets her brain at zero and curls around his legs like a cat. It really porks me."

Gram's lips twitched. "And you—what do you do, around a boy?"

"I haven't been around any, not in the sense Anne is. Not so they'd *notice*, I mean. I told you, I'm backward."

"You'll catch up."

"Oh sure," said Jimmie without conviction. She sighed gustily. "Maybe I should be glad, just to be marking time for a while. Sometimes, when I look ahead, when I see where I'm heading—I wish I could go into reverse."

"I guess we all feel that at times, and at any age," Gram said. She placed her fingers to her temples, and Jimmie, with a start of panic, saw that the hands were shaking slightly. When Gram looked ahead and saw where *she* was heading—

"Gram!" She threw her arms around this older—not really old at all—person she loved. "Gram, you stop that!"

Her grandmother smiled, and shook her head as if in self-reproach. "How foolish of me. Come along, Jimmie dear. Help me put your father's shirts away."

They went down the hall, Jimmie still shaken at that sudden unbidden glimpse of—of Death. *Seeing that death, a necessary end, Will come when it will come.* That was from Julius Caesar, and it had come to him, and would even to her Gram, and to herself.

Death.

Gram knocked on her father's study door, though they both knew he was at the office. Gram never went into a room without knocking, and she had once told Jimmie a most peculiar fact—how, in olden days, and not so long ago olden, even, servants in superior hotels and in the mansions of the rich never knocked on doors. They simply entered, did what they came to do, and left. Because servants, as people, as observers or reacting human beings, were held not to exist, so there was nothing for them to observe or react to, no matter *what* was going on. She had actually heard Marcy Beggs's mother referring

to a maid's becoming "uppity, forgetting her place." It
had seemed to Jimmie so quaint a phrase that she'd wanted
to laugh. Well, if you knew about things like that—servants not knocking on doors—you'd have to say the
world had progressed some. Nobody these days, no matter how rich and important, nobody, not even the Beggs
family, could get away with pretending that somebody
who worked for them didn't exist and couldn't react.
That was the sort of thing her mother ought to concentrate on once in a while, instead of on everything that
was wrong with society. Not that that was such a great
leap forward, or anything, but just the same they hadn't
stood *still* in those times. We've advanced a *little,* Jimmie
thought.

They went into the study that smelled of pipe tobacco
and wood and glue. Dad had a big desk on which he put
his carving things. He made, with his thin gifted fingers,
marvelous little creatures of wood. Tiny birds to hang on
the boughs of a Christmas tree, their little feathers mirac-
ulously distinct, each bird painted with a minute delicate
brush in bright clear colors. He was carving a chess set
now.

"Look at the king," said Jimmie, picking it up. "Isn't
he imposing?"

The king—no way of knowing yet if he was the black
king or the white, since, as her father said, the painting
of this chess set lay far in the future—was six inches tall
and he sat upon a throne. Jimmie didn't think there was
another chess set in the world where the king and queen
were seated on thrones. "When you think about it logi-
cally," Dr. Gavin had said, "it isn't logical. How are they
supposed to get around the board while they're sitting
down?"

"Maybe courtiers are carrying them," Jimmie offered.

"That's a thought. But should I now plan to carve
courtiers?"

"Why don't you just be illogical? It *looks* grand."

"Isn't he elegant, Gram?" she said now.

"He certainly is." Gram gently touched the row of
pawns that were like faceless children with their hands
behind their backs. "Your father does this sort of thing so

beautifully. He always has. Even as a child. He was the only child I ever knew who whittled. I guess being a dentist was a sort of natural outcome. Even though," she added in a tone of unaccustomed brittleness, "your Grandmother Prior considers it a revolting trade. Poking around in strangers' mouths, I heard her say once. She didn't even refer to it as a profession."

"Oh now, Gram," Jimmie said uncomfortably. "You know Grandmother. Don't get upset. She just says things."

"Doesn't she just."

"Have you seen Daddy's new assistant?" Jimmie asked, to change the subject.

"Briefly, that day she was here."

"She's an awful lot younger than Miss Kavanagh." Not liking that as an alternate subject, she hurried on. "Speaking of the Lib, why is it women always turn out to be assistants and technicians and nurses and—handmaidens? Practically never the real thing."

"There are lots of women doctors. And lawyers."

"Are there any women dentists?"

"I'm sure there are."

"Now, you tell me, Gram. I want your honest opinion. Would you go to a lady dentist?"

"I would, *if* I thought she were qualified," Gram said, in a good imitation of her son's voice.

They were laughing when Mrs. Gavin came into the study, yawning and stretching her arms above her head. She wore a pink cashmere robe that fell in gentle folds to her ankles and had silken tassels on the belt.

All dressed up and no place to go but back to bed, Jimmie thought, irritated almost beyond endurance and having to harden herself against remorse at her own irritation. Maybe she's sick or something, the thought occurred. But that thought had occurred in the past, and to Dr. Gavin, too. Mrs. Gavin had had two or three workups at the hospital, to enable doctors to get at the cause of her sleeplessness, her unending fatigue. They'd never been able to find it. Her mother seemed to enjoy her stay at the hospital, and then came home and continued as before.

"What are you laughing at?" she asked now, shrugging

indifferently when a confused pause made it clear that neither her daughter nor her mother-in-law was prepared to say what they'd been laughing at.

Are we supposed to tell her that we've been kind of making fun of her husband? Jimmie thought. No, we aren't in the least required to tell her that. Because what Gram and I feel when we're laughing at him and what Mother seems to feel when she laughs at him are quite different things.

There were times when Mother seemed almost to wish to show Dad up in a bad, or ridiculous, light. To find him out in some little vanity or imposture.

Dr. Gavin would say something like, "That was in my Sir Thomas More period," and his wife would look up alertly and ask, "Your Sir Thomas More period? When was that?"

"Oh, I don't recall exactly, but I was very involved in reading his books and his life. A really great man."

"What did you read?"

"Well—I can't recall now. As I say, it was a long time ago."

"You didn't say. You said 'you didn't recall exactly.' But I should think that anyone who'd actually had a Sir Thomas More *period*—goodness, how fascinating that sounds—would remember when it was. Or at least what he'd read."

"I read his *Urn Burial*, of course."

"*Urn Burial*. Surely that was written by Sir Thomas Browne? You must be thinking of More's *Utopia*."

"Of course I was thinking of *Utopia*. I read *Urn Burial* at about the same time." Dr. Gavin would be beginning to sound edgy, but since he never lost his temper or walked out of a room in a rage, he was, in a sense, at bay, as it became clear that if he'd ever actually had a Sir Thomas More period, it had entirely left his memory.

"Goodness, you've read them both. I've never read either. Tell me about *Utopia*," Mrs. Gavin would pursue, not caring, Jimmie came to realize, who else was present besides her husband and herself.

In fact, at such a time, there was, for them, no one else present. They were alone, pretending to talk about

Sir Thomas More, but saying something quite different. As if her father said, "I'm someone with scholarly interests, not just a second-rate suburban dentist with my fingers in other people's mouths," and her mother replied, "Don't put on airs in front of me, because I'll unmask you."

"No, but really," she'd press on, "tell me about More's *Utopia.* I've always been interested in it but never enough, I fear, to make a study of it, as you have. What is it, generally speaking?"

"What is any book about Utopia about? It concerned an ideal state?"

"Well, of course. Only, what was his particular vision of the ideal state?"

These conversations, which usually took place at the dinner table, since that was the only time when they were all together, were never concluded. Goya, who, unless he was having a story read to him, rarely listened to what anyone else was saying, would surface from some inner pool with an irrelevant question. "How do birds protect themselves from the rain?" he'd ask, and Dr. and Mrs. Gavin would quickly turn their attention to him. Or Jimmie, embarrassed for her father and bewildered by her mother, would utter a shrill and unrelated comment meant to derail them, and it usually did. In a peculiar fashion—they, after all, were the ones conducting the acid exchange—they always welcomed a chance to cut it short. And, in a moment, Mrs. Gavin would be asking her husband if he'd had a good day, sounding pleasant and concerned, as if she really wished to know. Dr. Gavin would respond agreeably, and they'd go on as if no hostile emanations had flowed from them only moments before.

But why, Jimmie would ask herself, cautiously relaxing, why, if people could do this sort of thing to each other, did they get married in the first place? Why did her father talk about reading Sir Thomas More, when what he really liked was re-runs of *Gunsmoke?* Why did her mother take such almost cruel pleasure in exposing his pretense? And if that was necessary, what sort of relationship was it anyway? When she listened to her parents, or the parents of some of her friends, she could understand why young people now were suspicious of marriage. Suspicious, many of them, to the point of finding it too dangerous a venture to try.

"Well, I guess I'll leave you two," she heard her mother saying. "You seem to find enough to say to each other when I'm not here, so it's my presence has struck you dumb."

"You know that's not so," Gram protested, putting the shirts in one of the built-in drawers in the wall storage space that Dr. Gavin had built in here for himself. "We were just being silly."

"I see," Mrs. Gavin said in a wistful tone. She looked curiously around the room where for months now her husband had been spending his nights. Feeling, no doubt, that they had to explain the situation, Dr. Gavin had said that his wife's restless nights left him exhausted in the morning. "I can't go to work on two or three hours of sleep," he told Jimmie, who hadn't asked. "So it seems more sensible all around for me to stay in the study."

Jimmie, preferring not to think about the sexual part of her parents' life at all, or even if they had that part any more, mumbled something, she couldn't now remember what, and the matter had not been mentioned since.

"I guess you've taken care of his shirts again," Mrs. Gavin said to her mother-in-law.

"Just sewed on a few buttons—"

"Well, thank you."

"It's all right. I was glad to do it."

A stiff silence followed this stiff exchange, and then Mrs. Gavin, with a little gesture of the hand that she used to disassociate herself from the world and the people in it, left them.

Later, remembering how she'd said she couldn't talk with her mother, Jimmie had had a sad sense of disloyalty. If you couldn't have loyalty in a *family*, where would you ever find it? Okay, so her mother wouldn't talk personalities, yet it was to her mother Jimmie had first gone when a period of racial tension at school had made her sick, with fear and with shame.

"Shame?" her mother had said. "Did you align yourself on the white side?"

"I didn't align myself anywhere. I stayed out of the way and said nothing. Which is why I feel ashamed, don't you see."

"You know, I'm coming to believe that bigotry should be treated as a psychiatric problem. Scratch a bigot and you find an emotional cripple. My solution would be to set up treatment centers for bigots, the way we have for alcoholics and drug addicts. Of course, we spend almost nothing on those, either. Money in this country is used principally to devise methods of destroying people, not helping them. . . ."

As usual, an attempt to talk about her subjective feelings had brought about an objective discussion of social ills, but nevertheless, when she was ashamed of her own behavior she could go to her mother and get, not reassurance, but anyway a serious hearing. So why didn't she value that more?

Her father, when she'd spoken of it to him, had said of course it was wrong, deplorable, but fortunately there was not much of that at her particular school, and when there was, she was to *stay out of it*.

"Do you want me to be a coward, Daddy?"

"I want you to be safe, period."

Well, that hadn't been what she wanted to hear, either. She didn't know what she wanted to hear, unless it was for someone to tell her that the world's griefs and wrongs had been exaggerated to begin with and would be over shortly anyway, by Washington's Birthday, at the very latest.

CHAPTER SEVEN

After Gram had gone, and with her the popovers, the cookies, the homemade bread—and something warmer, homier—life settled into the long end-of-winter period when winter finally does seem endless. School in the morning, home in the afternoon to a kitchenful of the breakfast dishes, the washer-dryer piled with clothes that were dirty and hadn't been washed yet, or clean and hadn't been sorted yet. Jimmie usually did the dishes and the laundry, just to get them out of the way. But sometimes, out of irritation, or spite, she left them there, and eventually her mother got around to doing them.

The walk to the bus in the morning, and the bus itself, with its three puny little heaters, seemed to grow worse as January slushed its way into February, and February fell like a corpse across the path of March.

Jimmie, formulating this melodramatic metaphor, arrived at the bus stop one morning to find Anne Ferris missing. Late, she thought, surprised. She looked down the street, expecting at any moment to see her friend come running toward her. But when Dick pulled up, there was still no Anne, and Jimmie boarded, looking over her shoulder.

"Where's your little friend?" Dick asked. "Anne, isn't it?"

Jimmie thought how pleased Anne was going to be to hear he had asked for her. Anne could maintain a level

of romantic concentration that was awesome, and somehow in spite of his complete unawareness of it, continued
to suffer over and rejoice in Dick.

"I don't know," she said. "She isn't sick, I shouldn't
think. I mean, we talked on the telephone for an hour last
night and she sounded fine then."

"Oh well. Overslept, probably."

Anne never oversleeps, Jimmie thought. But Dick was
pulling up for the jocks, who greeted him with shouted
insults that somehow came out to affection. One thing, at
least, this winter, Jimmie thought, settling by a window to
study the cold passing landscape, one thing to be thankful
for and that was that Dick had tamed the hoody element
on his bus to such a point that the only real discomfort
now was the chill of the ride. And even that gave way to
close, unpleasant warmth as more and more kids piled
aboard at each stop.

She held her books on her lap. At her feet was a little
petit-point overnight case, worked by Grandmother Prior,
in which were the things she'd meant to take to Anne's
after school. What she wondered was, was she still to
spend the night at the Ferrises'? Last night, on the telephone, Anne had sounded fine and looking forward to her
visit.

"We can talk and play records and you can take Father's mind off Peter," Anne had said, and when Jimmie
inquired why that was necessary, Anne had said that tomorrow (today) was Peter's birthday, and their father
was in one of his moods for exhorting his son to pull
himself together and find an aim in life. Peter was in college and had had five majors so far.

"But, Anne—I'm not so sure I should *be* there on Peter's birthday," Jimmie had protested. "Isn't it better to
keep it a family thing?"

"On the contrary. You'll be just the ticket for keeping
things calm. A drop of oil on troubled waters, that's what
you'll be."

Jimmie had let herself be persuaded, as she could usually be by anyone who was persuasive enough, but she
admitted to herself a feeling now of relief that apparently
the visit was off. She hoped nothing catastrophic had hap-

pened at the Ferrises' to keep Anne away from school, but for her part she was glad that at the day's end she'd be going home where the waters were, just at present, not troubled enough to require oil.

Anne, of course, was probably exaggerating as usual. She liked to "heighten life's hues" as she put it. Her family was one of the closest-knit Jimmie had ever known. Mr. and Mrs. Ferris were enough to make a girl believe in marriage, and it wasn't that they fell over each other. They just seemed to belong together.

But I wonder, she thought, as the bus went past an old disused town graveyard, if there are any families where the waters are always calm and clear right down to the bottom. Probably not. Probably it would be a bore if—

She scrunched her right arm close to her body because the character next to her was trying to nudge her breast, all the while talking to someone across the aisle as if he didn't know what he was doing.

Pig, thought Jimmie, without much heat. This sort of thing, and a bit worse, happened on the bus from time to time and you only made things worse by protesting. She even had an impulse to giggle. What if she said to him in a loud voice, "You must be pretty hard up, if my chest gives you a throb. Why don't you come around again in about a year?" That'd fix him, but good. And earn her a two-hundred-pound enemy.

Better to do nothing, think about something else.

That old graveyard back there. She could remember when, a few years ago, riding this same bus route that she'd ridden since the first grade, she'd had to close her eyes before they came to it, and then hope she wouldn't inadvertently open them before the danger of seeing the thin old leaning grave markers, the stone angels and crosses, was past.

But last fall Anne and Marcy Beggs had suggested one day that they walk around the churchyard, reading the markers, and Jimmie hadn't objected. She'd long since got over shivering at the sight of the little cemetery. It was so old. It was sort of touching. Except for when someone left a jar of flowers—fake or real—or a potted plant, from time to time, nothing new or fresh ever happened there, or had for ages.

"It gives you a sort of per*spec*tive," Anne had said, moseying down the rows of gravestones, stopping now and then to read an epitaph. Some of them were almost indecipherable. "I mean, you realize that somebody's *down* there, right under our feet. Or anyway their bones are, or something is. And it was somebody just as alive as we are now. It makes it—I don't know—more *rea*sonable, more everyday, to think about dying. I mean, that's how it takes me."

Marcy had nodded. She was a strange wonderful girl that Jimmie was proud to have for a friend. Taller than any other girl in the school. Taller than any of the boys, except the very biggest. With a lovely face and lots of long brown gleaming hair and gentle ways. It was as if, at her cradle, the good fairies, the ones who'd been invited, had said, "We'll give her beauty and charm and brains and wealth and the gift of making friends," and had felt that they'd certainly covered every contingency, as good fairies strive to do. But the wicked *un*invited fairy had hurled in at the last moment, cackling, "I'll give her incredible height *and* insecurity." Therefore Marcy walked through life stoop-shouldered, with a kind of stalking, storklike gait, and was never sure of her welcome though she was welcome everywhere.

She had stopped at a graying, lichen-stippled marker.

"This is a great-great-great-great-great aunt of mine," she said. The Beggs family had lived in these parts since the 17th century and you ran into the name all over the place. Beggs Hardware. Beggs and Wylie, Solicitors. Beggs Lumberyard. The Beggs Building, which was in the middle of downtown and was the professional building where doctors and dentists had their offices. Jimmie's father's office was in the Beggs Building.

"Look at what it says," Marcy asked them, though of course she herself knew what some old-time stone carver, long gone himself, had chiseled on this plain granite marker.

Elspeth Spooner Beggs, Wife of Gordon Beggs, 1841, Aet. 67 years, 4 months, 7 days. *She Did Her Best*.

"Pretty negative," Jimmie commented. "Couldn't your great-great-great-great-great uncle have done better by her?"

"Maybe it was all he could think of. Maybe she led him a merry dance—or a miserable dance—all his life, and when she died he couldn't think of anything better than that to put about her."

"Better not to say anything, if you ask me," Jimmie decided.

They'd wandered on, reaching out tentative fingers now and then to touch a leaning tombstone, sharing a sense of youth and aliveness and, in truth, immortality, here in this place where so many old old people, who had nothing to do with them, with now, had their mortality etched.

"Look at this," Anne had said, stooping to read the legend under a carved stone cherub whose wings and features had been eroded to smoothness by time and the weather.

Willow Farnham, Died March 25, 1868, Aged 16. *Her family loved her, but Jesus loved her more.*

"Sixteen," Anne had breathed. "Only sixteen."

"What a very very pretty name," Jimmie said, in the same sighing tone. "Willow Farnham."

Willow's tomb was at the edge of the cemetery, in a corner, next to a stand of sugar maples, beyond which was an apple orchard. Jimmie wondered if the orchard had been there when Willow died, and imagined it must have been. The maples were old, maybe had been saplings a hundred years before Willow was born.

The three of them had left the cemetery by the orchard and had walked the two miles to town, where they'd gone to the Beggs Building to see if Dr. Gavin could give them a ride home. They'd hardly spoken, but Jimmie was sure that Anne and Marcy too were netted in perplexed and vaporous imaginings about Willow Farnham, who'd been loved, and only sixteen, when she died. Dying seemed such an old person's thing to do. Or, at any rate, a grown-up thing. But of course you knew it was something anyone of any age could do. All you had to do, to bring it off, was be alive.

"You know," said a sharp voice in her ear. "I've been sitting next to you for ten minutes and you haven't said word one."

Jimmie turned. Faith Powers, looking aggrieved, as always.

"I thought you were a football player."

"You what?"

Jimmie stifled a laugh. "Not really. I was trying to be funny. But there was one of those tacky tackle types here, trying to—you know—paw me."

"Yeah? What'd you do?"

"I said, 'Eff off, you male chauvinist pig!' "

"Did you, honestly?"

"No. Just thought it. And then I didn't notice when he left. Where'd he get to?"

"Search me. I saw this seat up front and grabbed it. I don't like it back there."

"Who does."

"Where's Anne?"

"I don't know. She wasn't at the bus stop. And I'm supposed to spend the night with her, too." As she spoke, she wished she hadn't. Faith led a lonely social life, and Jimmie was sorry for her. Not sorry enough to do much about it, except be friendly at school. But you didn't want to go around hurting people's feelings.

"I mean, we have to plan some stuff for her brother's birthday—" She stopped, realizing that explanations were only going to make matters worse.

"Barfy day," Faith grumbled. "I can't stand this cold weather. I think I may go to Bermuda at Easter."

"That'd be nice."

"We have these friends there who have this seaside house. I want to tell you, it's something else. And they're always asking us down so my folks said let's just go this year instead of always talking about it and never doing it. I, for one, can hardly wait to get away from everybo—everything. The cold, and all."

"That'd be nice," Jimmie repeated, and wondered why it was that no matter what Faith was talking about, it bored. Faith was absolutely the most tedious human being she had ever in her life encountered. She was such a bore that she frightened a listener into wondering if she mightn't be one, too. If Faith couldn't recognize such a noticeable characteristic in herself, maybe no one else could either? Still, it didn't seem right to dislike somebody for a reason like that. You could not like them because they were cruel, or brutish, or gross. Faith was none of those, and that she wearied a person senseless with her dull dumb talk did not seem fair or adequate grounds for dislike.

Attempting to look alert, pleasant, and credulous as Faith described the house in Bermuda and the joys that lay in wait there for the Powers family (there was a boy —a dreamboat—and a boat—a sailboat—and there was to be scuba diving and snorkeling and dancing on the moonlit patio), Jimmie strangled a yawn.

"That should be nice," she said in a lengthening pause during which she realized that she was expected to comment. Did boring people make bores of their listeners? It would seem so.

At school, as she was shoving jacket, mittens, and boots into her locker, and changing to loafers because she couldn't wear boots all day the way some girls did—they made her feet itch—Anne arrived, breathing hard.

"Thought I'd be late," she said, getting out her comb. "Father drove me because I missed the bus. There was a passage of arms over Peter's birthday and we all forgot the time."

"What happened?"

"*Well*," said Anne. "You going to study hall first? Good. Well, let me *tell* you," and she launched on the scenario.

It seemed that at breakfast Anne's mother had said to her husband, "Guess what Peter wants for his birthday?"

"A pound of pot?"

"Don't make jokes like that," Mrs. Ferris had said sharply.

"I wish I knew I was joking. What does he want?"

"He'd like us to take him out to dinner. To a restaurant."

Mr. Ferris had looked across the table at his wife,

shaken his head and buttered a piece of toast.

"If you're waiting for my answer," he'd said after a while, "if you can't guess it, well, the answer is no. I am not going out before the community gaze with Peter."

"But Vincent—he hasn't asked for anything else. Not one other thing."

"I'll give him anything else. Just tell him to say the word. Not to exceed, of course, our life savings, and whatever I can get by mortgaging the house, and—"

"Oh, Vincent—stop. Don't tease. This is important to him."

"He's testing us, dear. Don't you get it? He's setting us tasks. Herculean tasks. I'm not Hercules."

Peter, during this exchange, had still been in bed. As Anne said, he stayed up half the night looking at late movies and then sacked out most of the following day. "It drives Father absolutely bananas. He says just to *think* of that great hulk lying in bed while everyone else is up and working throws him right through the ceiling. Mother said shouldn't Peter be able to rest when he was home from college, and Father said since he spent the school year resting on his D's, he damn well ought to work when he was home."

"I don't care if he cleans the garage or paints the basement. In fact, I don't care if he does nothing but get out of bed and stand on his feet," Mr. Ferris had said. "Just so he doesn't *rest*."

Peter had been home from college for a week of intersession, and had worn every day a pair of dungarees stapled up one leg, a plaid shirt with part of a sleeve missing and a strange growth of beard that wasn't really a beard at all, Anne said, but just looked like a face that hadn't been shaven for several days. Nobody could figure how he kept it at just that certain state of dishevelment.

"I think," Mr. Ferris had said, "that he shaves and then pastes those goddam whiskers on."

They wouldn't ask him about it, just as they had kept to a pact, concluded by Anne's mother and father, not to comment on Peter's clothing or his choice of food. It was their new approach, and seemed to be working no better than the old one (nagging).

"What it comes to," Mrs. Ferris had said this morning, "is that you're ashamed of your son. And don't tell me you're not because I wouldn't believe it."

"I wasn't going to tell you I'm not, because I am. I'm ashamed of the way he looks. It's embarrassing."

"If you love someone, looks should be beside the question."

"You don't catch me that way, friend. I draw the line at appearing with someone who looks—who looks like Pete. *And* who might order a bowl of sunflower seeds for dinner, for all we know. I do love him. He looks like a cross between Karl Marx and a long-needled pine, he talks like a damned anarchist, and if he isn't on grass I'll eat the lawn. But I love him. We'll eat at home."

"So, what are you going to do?" Jimmie asked.

"You mean what are *we* going to do, because you're coming home with me and that's that. I don't know. Nothing was settled when we tore out of the house and Father just muttered all the way to school. Clutching, isn't it?"

When school let out they were walking toward the line of buses when Anne grabbed Jimmie's arm and let out a yelp. "Lookit, Jimmie! There's Peter, and he's talking to Dick! He *knows* him. Come *on*, Jimmie—"

The two young men were leaning against Dick's bus, talking.

". . . so I drive the bus mornings and afternoons, grab a quick snooze in between, drive to New York to the hiring hall, get a cab, and cruise till eleven," Dick was saying. "I tell you, Pete, you should see that garage where we wait to see if we'll get a hack. Everyone with hair to here sitting around reading Hermann Hesse and Thucydides. Not everyone, of course. Some of the Old Guard are still there, glaring."

"You get a job every time?"

"They're hurting for drivers in New York. I could hack twenty-four hours a day, if there was some way to get around sleeping. What're you doing, Pete?"

"Home for intersession." Peter Ferris frowned. "I don't know for a fact what I'm doing. Far as school goes, I'm still hanging in. It's not the best scene, but since there's only this one more semester to go, I might as well tie it up. For some reason my father still thinks a college degree matters, and for some reason what my father thinks still matters to me. I may go to Europe in the summer. I did last year."

"That's what I figure on doing. Earn enough bread to get to the British Isles. Friend of mine has been walking all over Ireland and Wales for nearly a year. I figure I could meet up with him and keep walking. He says you can get by on forty bucks a week. That's why I'm working this way, killing myself so I can lay off for a couple of years." Dick glanced at Anne and Jimmie. "Hop on, kiddies. Ready to roll in a couple of minutes."

Anne looked eagerly at her brother, who seemed to snap out of a reverie and said, "Dick, this is my kid sister, Anne. And her friend, Ji—"

"Janine Gavin," said Anne. "Peter, I didn't know you two knew each other."

"Went to Hotchkiss together," Dick said. "I'm so much older than your brother here that we never got to know each other too well."

"He's two years older," said Peter. "Time erases these gaps."

"This is Peter's birthday, so now you're only a year older," said Anne, ignoring her brother's exasperated glance. She said, "Did they decide about taking you out to dine, Peter? That's what he wants for his birthday," she said to Dick.

"Strange wish."

"Father says Peter is setting them tasks. Is that true, Pete?"

"Could be."

"They're ashamed of his appearance," Anne explained.

"Why?" said Dick, looking the other boy up and down. They bore a resemblance to each other, and in this bore a resemblance to many other young men their age. Shabbily dressed, as if much deliberation had gone into it, long-haired, unselfconscious about it. But Jimmie, looking from one to the other, felt a spurt of sympathy for Peter's father. Dick, with his thick burnished hair cut like Harry Hotspur's, was presentable in spite of his clothes.

Peter's hair was a fright wig of tangled black Medusa curls, and his attempt at a beard looked like strands of spiderweb stuck to a little cushion.

Still, they were both marvelous, and for herself, she wouldn't be ashamed to be seen with either one of them.

"My old man," Peter was saying, "will spend hours talking with me at home, trying to find out what's going on in my head. He's great that way, even if he says that one of America's great contributions to culture was to formulate the generation gap. He says it should be kept as wide as possible. But then he'll stay up till two closing it by listening to me. But, man, he wouldn't walk to the mailbox with me if there was anyone around. They're screwed up, but good. Did you hear that Dusty Potter's father threw him out of the house?"

"Yeah, I heard about it. Where's old Dusty now?"

"In a commune, somewhere in Oregon. He's an itinerant carpenter, or fruit picker, or something."

"I don't think I could go all the way back to nature that way."

"If you're going to walk around Wales and Ireland, you'll be back to nature, son. I went to Ireland last year and there's nothing between here and Dublin City but a bog and a few sheep dogs rounding up their flocks. I really dug it."

"Let's get together and talk about it, right? Okay, okay," Dick shouted to his now filled bus. "Right with you. You girls coming?"

"No, I came over to pick them up," Peter said, gesturing toward the school parking lot. "They're going to help me do the marketing."

Dick got into the bus, settled in the driver's seat and leaned out the window, his left hand lifted, "Peace," he said.

"Peace," said Peter, and smiled at the girls. "To the market now, okay?"

CHAPTER EIGHT

The Ferrises, their house, their dog, their lawn and garden were all crisp and clean and straightforwardly middle class. Mr. Ferris, who had a Ph.D. and was entitled to be called Dr. Ferris, but wasn't, taught European history at a small nearby college, where his wife taught French and wasn't entitled to be called doctor. He was on the local school board and she on the Fair Housing Committee for the county. They went abroad together once every three years, read interesting periodicals ranging from *The Village Voice* to *The National Review* (so as to get the whole picture, they said). They enjoyed skiing, ballet, sailing, and each other. They enjoyed their children's friends and there was usually company of various ages at their house.

Mrs. Ferris shared the current desperation of American housewives—whether to pollute the air, the ground, the lakes, the sea a little, a lot, or how much and what would. Whether to buy organic (and believe you were actually getting it) and toss out the MSG, or feed your family just a little poison, since the food tasted so much better that way, and anyway who knew what you were using today that tomorrow would be suspect and what you were not using today that tomorrow would be back in the good graces of the FDA? Whether to throw out the dishwasher, beat the egg whites by hand, and go back to napkin rings, or just ban plastic wrap and aluminum foil

72

from your shelves. Mrs. Ferris had in her closet an alligator bag and a coat with a red fox collar that she would neither wear nor give away, and she'd been known to burst into tears over the morning mail which consisted of 99 per cent requests or pleas for money and all for purposes that seemed not only valid but urgent.

"What does *your* mother do about all this?" she'd appealed to Jimmie once.

"Well, let's see. We've been using soap now for several years. We're only allowed four inches of water for a bath, or a five-minute shower, and we can't run it while we brush our teeth. The dishwasher broke last year and that's that—we aren't getting a new one. And mother—she's just never *worn* fur or animal skins. Not since I've known her."

"She was in the vanguard, all right," Mrs. Ferris said in a tone that mixed admiration and annoyance about equally.

She did not pursue the matter of the mails, and Jimmie didn't volunteer the fact that in their house her mother was always trying to send checks to peace organizations, organizations to improve the quality of Congress, wildlife organizations, civil rights organizations, organizations to protect the legal rights of the poor, and some others that she'd forgotten, and her father was always trying to keep these donations within reason. His reason, of course. Still, her father was a man with a social conscience, and he did contribute as much as he thought they could.

"But we *could* give more," her mother had said one day. "I mean, it isn't as if we spent much on ourselves. We don't even go on vacations."

"And whose fault is it that we don't go on vacations?" he'd demanded.

"That isn't the point. The point is that since we don't—"

Jimmie had left without waiting for her mother to get to the point. Beleaguered, that's what they all seemed to her.

Today, when Anne and Jimmie arrived at the Ferrises' with Peter and several sacks of groceries, Mrs. Ferris was in the kitchen preparing a shrimp casserole.

"I see," said Peter, lugging in the last of the grocery bags. "I get it. We're eating home."

"Nope. This is for the freezer. Hello, Jimmie dear—how nice to have you here for Peter's birthday. At least, I hope it'll be nice. You may wish you'd stayed home. We are all," she said, a little loudly, "going out to dine, as it is Peter's birthday wish and we try not to deny him his wishes. Of course, his father has a short fuse, as Peter well knows, and we can only pray that no—incidents occur."

"Why should an incident occur?" Peter asked happily. "Say, that's neat of you and Father. In a way, I suppose I should let you out of it, now that he's said yes. But it'll be an experience for all of us."

"That's what I'm afraid of," said Mrs. Ferris, but she didn't sound alarmed, and she looked at her rumpled hairy son with great fondness.

He picked a mushroom out of the casserole and said as he chewed it, "Say, I notice you're using soap now, and that's fine, but you had paper towels on the list. I didn't get them. Good old cloth towels, that's the ticket."

"Peter—" Mrs. Ferris began, but gave a helpless little laugh and said, "All right, all right, from now on no paper towels. I thought you just meant not colored paper towels, because of the dye or whatever it is."

"Well, the colored kind is worse, but all these things have junk on them to make them strong that isn't biodegradable. We shouldn't use any paper that isn't absolutely necessary." He took another mushroom. "I know a guy in Vermont, Mother, who built his new house without a bathroom." He smiled at the recollection. "His mother came up to visit him and in a while asked for what I think she'd have called 'the conveniences.' He told her there weren't any, in the sense she was speaking of, but there were a hundred acres of woods and meadow outside."

"Good heavens," said Mrs. Ferris, closing her eyes. "What did the poor woman do?"

"Said, 'Well then, where's the toilet tissue?' She's okay."

"But is her son? Okay? He sounds like a nut."

"No, when you think it over, he makes sound ecological sense. He's going to build an outhouse one of these days, of course."

"How very advanced."

"Don't knock it. You realize how much water he saves not flushing toilets all the time? To say nothing of no septic tank to carry sewage and phosphates and caustics and all the other laundry junk right into the streams and rivers of Vermont?"

"How does he bathe?" Mrs. Ferris asked coldly.

"Oh well, Mother—if you're going to nitpick."

"Peter, I know that you bathe when you're home. But when you're up there in school, I can only rely on your training to make you observe fundamental—" She broke off, looking at the two girls and realized she'd strayed too far into the realm of the personal. "Oh, dear," she sighed. "Help me put the groceries away, somebody."

"Beleaguered," said Jimmie, lounder than she'd planned to. They all turned to her. "That's what I think people are. Beleaguered. Everybody."

"That about sums it up," said Mrs. Ferris.

That evening Peter came down for the outing dressed in pants that were old but had no obvious rips or patches, a turtleneck sweater, and an old tweed jacket. He'd shaved off his strange whiskers. Clearly, he had made an effort.

Mr. Ferris, too, made an effort.

Everyone in the car sensed at what cost to his nervous system he drove to a respectable restaurant and not to a nearby dive or diner. Everyone, Jimmie thought, except Peter, was taut and talkative during the drive.

"*I* remember," said Mrs. Ferris, "when what were called 'respectable places' wouldn't let a man in without a jacket and tie. Remember, dear," she said, turning to her husband, "that place that time where the headwaiter tried to make you put on a *paper* jacket? It was summer," she explained to the others. "And hot. Your father just had on a knit shirt—a very nice shirt, of course. But that's the way it was in those days."

"What did Father do?" Peter asked, smiling.

"Oh now, can you imagine anybody di*rect*ing your father to put on this paper jacket or no din-din? He said something quite vulgar to the headwaiter and we went someplace else, or went hungry, I can't recall."

"If it's my turtleneck brought on this fine recollection," Peter said, "don't give it another thought, Mother. I'll pass muster anywhere."

Mr. Ferris glanced in the rearview mirror at his son, whose hair stood up in a great dingy halo, and who met his glance with an expression of guileless happiness. "You know, Father, you and Mother should make more of an effort to catch up with the times. She tells me it's so long since you've been to a movie that you've never even seen a naked body on the screen."

"We didn't like movies when there weren't any naked bodies on it," Mr. Ferris muttered. "No reason to go now, just because there are."

"No, but that's one of the things I mean. Our movies show what we *are*, to a great extent. Open and honest— about nakedness in part, of course, but not just nakedness of the body. We're trying to strip the human mind of its pretentious coverings, too."

"Who's we?"

"Me. People my age. The kids' age, here, too. People your students' age. You'd have a better insight into the people you're teaching if you listened to our music and saw the kind of shows we like."

"I don't have to listen to all that caterwauling or turn voyeur in order to lecture on the Congress of Vienna. And were young people always so pompously possessive? *Our* movies, *our* music—"

"Yes," said his wife. "We were."

"Father, you are *wrong*. Why, even to use the word *lecture* is recidivist of you."

"It's not recidivist, because I've always called what I do lecturing, and I don't think you know what the word means anyway. Recidivism is relapsing into criminal habits. I have no criminal habits."

"I think it's criminal to call what you do lecturing. And it's selling yourself short, too. You're a good teacher, but I sometimes think that maybe you could've even been great, if you'd been more with it." Peter pondered. "Not too late, even now."

"Well, thanks for the encouragement. But I have sufficient insight into my students to get them interested in what de Tocqueville had to say about America and fascinated at how much of it came to pass. Some of them. Some of them wouldn't be interested in Armageddon if they were on the field. And I don't want to be a great teacher."

"Now, come *on*, Father. How can you say a thing like that?"

"I just put one word after another word and it comes out to something like that."

"Yeah, but you don't mean—"

"*Here* we are," said Mr. Ferris, swinging into the parking area of a French country restaurant that had an awning outside and a maître d' inside who looked at them cordially until his glance rested on Peter, when his expression chilled.

"This way, sir," he said to Mr. Ferris, leading them to a secluded table near the kitchen and thrusting menus at them with something less than a flourish.

Mr. Ferris' expression became even icier than that of the maître d' and he opened his mouth to say something that Jimmie was sure would result in an open confrontation. She looked with some alarm at Anne, who seemed merely attentive, then at Peter, who was eyeing his father with lively interest.

Mrs. Ferris said, "This will do nicely, *won't* it, Vincent?"

Another hesitation, and the maître d' pulled out Mrs. Ferris' chair for her with a slight increase in courtesy.

I guess, Jimmie thought, he saw the look in Mr. Ferris' eye, too. It would take somebody awfully brave to risk rousing a man with that expression to further anger.

Then they were seated. Jimmie held the menu, which was all in French, in hands that shook slightly, and suddenly she felt a slight pressure from Mrs. Ferris' hand. "How good is your French, Jimmie?" she asked. "Shall I interpret for you?"

Jimmie let out a breath she hadn't realized she'd been holding. "I think I can manage. I've been taking French for three years."

They concentrated on ordering, and Peter, as Anne had predicted, asked for the vegetable dinner. Informed by their waiter that there was no vegetable dinner, he patiently explained that one could be made up by eliminating the meat from his dish. "Or the fish, if you prefer," he said. "Eliminate either one you want and put on an extra vegetable. Simple as that," he said, handing his menu back to the waiter, who, for a fractional moment, rested his glance—contemptuous or antagonistic, it was hard to tell—on Peter's wild head of hair. Then, encountering Mrs. Ferris' eye, in which she put a great deal of hauteur and authority, he agreed that a vegetable dinner could, after all, probably be managed.

While Mr. and Mrs. Ferris had a martini each, and Anne and Jimmie ginger ale (Peter sipped at his glass of water), Jimmie looked furtively at the other tables to see if there was anyone else who looked as kooky as Peter or as testy as his father. There were so many long-haired young men and boys in the country today—there were a few in high school who wore ponytails—that it seemed silly for everyone to get so exercised over Peter's crazy coiffure. Of course, his great ball of matted curls was crazier than most.

Besides, anybody would know that it wasn't just Peter's hair that bugged his father. It was Peter. It was Peter's refusal to want or respect the things that Mr. Ferris, and his wife, thought mattered, like schooling or cleanliness or preparing to take his place in the world.

And Peter poked and prodded like a picador. Only this morning he'd told Dick he planned to finish the semester and get his degree, because it would please his father, and now he was saying in an idle tone that perhaps he'd split for Colorado and the ski slopes after intersession.

"What's the point in hanging around for a B.A. that I'm never going to have any use for anyway?" he asked, prodding, prodding his father, who, after his martini, seemed more relaxed. "I mean, if I had any aspiration to make my way up the organization ladder, that'd be one thing—"

"Your plans are to climb down, right?" said Mr. Ferris.

"Well, if you want to put it that way."

"I suppose," Mr. Ferris mused, "that this—downward social mobility, I guess you'd call it—that's occurring among young men and women is legitimate enough, in your own view. You say you want no part of the corporate structure, or of the establishment, or the military, so you all go out and drive taxis or work on garbage trucks or retire to Vermont and live organically and unhygienically. But what's going to happen to society if you all cop out this way?"

He was not, Jimmie thought, going to rise to Peter's bait about leaving school. She listened to the two of them talk, with an occasional comment from Mrs. Ferris as they turned to her. She and Anne just smiled when politely included by a glance. But the conversation really was Peter's and his father's.

"Society," said Peter, "is going to blow itself up, or it's going to breed itself out of existence, or choke to death on its products, and waste products."

"That's your answer."

"You've got the means to do it, any of those ways."

"You say 'You've got the means.' You aren't part of this society?"

"Not me. Not the people I know."

"That isn't my notion of courage."

"Who's talking about courage? We just want to feel a bit of peace, look at something beautiful and natural, work with our hands, read some good books and listen to music, and not kill anything, not in war, and not to eat or to wear. What is your idea of courage, Father?"

"Oh—" They'd arrived at coffee, and Mr. Ferris rather wearily drained his cup. "Standing for something, I guess. Knowing, for one thing, that acts have consequences, and being willing to take the consequences when you act. Those marches you went on. Those busts at the college you people took part in. Vandalizing books and papers, destroying the scholarship of years, beating up teachers, stoning policemen, and then whining for amnesty. Mobs. There's no such thing as a courageous mob, and you were all in mobs. Courage is an individual thing."

"And the police?" Peter said seriously. "The National

Guard? With the guns and tear gas and nightsticks. Their killings. You're letting them off?"

"They were mobs, too. Usually young men in a panic, or a rage, same as yourselves. Uncontrolled. Uncontrollable. It's all—it's all beyond words, beyond comprehending. It's—" He stopped, not equal to saying what he thought.

"So," said Peter, "the busts are over, and as far as I can make out, the marches, too. That crowd in Washington *conned* the Peace Movement to death. And I want to tell you something, Father, the marches *weren't* just mobs. They were a lot of individual people bearing physical witness to something they believed in. Peace among men. Love in the world. Brotherhood. The most exalting thing I ever did in my life was march for peace."

"And get put in jail."

"Right. That was taking the consequences of my acts, wasn't it? Let me tell you something else, being in *jail* is an individual thing. I don't care how many other people are there with you."

"Okay," said Mr. Ferris. "I'll give you that. But, I repeat my question, how are you going to achieve peace among men and love in the world, if you won't take part in the world? You can't go off and till your own garden, or drive your own hack, and stop the brutes at the top from brutalizing the world. You have to take your place in society and work there for something besides enough money to get to Europe for a year. *Or* Colorado for the skiing."

Peter leaned forward eagerly. "But, Father, look—" he began, and broke off as the waiter appeared beside them with the bill, and the conversation lapsed while Mr. Ferris paid and they prepared to leave.

As they passed a table near the doorway, a couple looked up at Peter and burst out laughing.

"Maybe they all aren't, but they all sure look like fags to me," said the man.

Vincent Ferris stopped as if braked. As he was leading the way, his wife, his son, his daughter and his daughter's friend were forced to halt behind him.

"Excuse me a moment," said Mr. Ferris. He turned and

walked slowly over to the couple, who abruptly ceased
to laugh. The woman looked apprehensive. The man, half-
risen from his chair, apprehensive and hostile. At the
door, the maître d' was looking furious and alarmed.

Mr. Ferris stood over the couple, studying them. With
his right index finger, he pushed the man's shoulder, hard.
The man swallowed noticeably, and sat down, his fists
clenched.

"You laughed," said Vincent Ferris.

"Yeah, you wanna—"

"You made an offensive comment."

"You wanna—"

"Don't laugh. Don't let your tongue wag. That boy is
mine. And it could happen to you." He continued to stare
down on them broodingly. "On second thought, I guess
it couldn't. Not to you two."

He rejoined his family and their guest and said cheer-
fully, "Well, shall we go home?"

CHAPTER NINE

On the drive through the dark and windy night back to the Ferrises', Anne's mother, twisting in the front seat to face them, said, "You girls have given Peter a nice present of allowing him and his father to do all the talking. Now, why don't you say something?"

"We like to hear Father and Peter settle the world from different directions," Anne answered for herself and Jimmie. "Anyway," she added, "Jimmie never has much to say. She's the quiet type."

Jimmie was going to protest this uncomplimentary compliment, but Anne was going on, "Father, I shall never ever forget you pushing that man into his seat with your pinky."

"It wasn't my—"

"You were super terrific. The upper*most*. Of course, we all thought coq au vin and demitasse were going to fly through the air, but I guess that man was a coward, don't you think?"

"I think he probably didn't want a public scene. Most people don't."

"Well, it was super, wasn't it, Pete?"

"Right on," said her brother. "Moving, that's what it was."

Mr. Ferris would not accept all this lying down. "It was a damn fool scene. *Moving*," he snorted. "I serve notice that from now on I plan to be an unmoved and detached observer of the passing scene where Peter and his whole generation are concerned. No interest, no involvement."

Peter was laughing as they drove into the garage and ran into the grateful warmth of their house. "You're the best, Father. By the way, I'm going back to school, you know. Just wanted to get you stirred up a bit."

"You frequently want to get me stirred up, though I fail to see why."

"Oh, it keeps the old juices flowing. I'm sorry I said what I said about your not being a great teacher—"

"Peter, I am not a great teacher," Mr. Ferris said in a tired voice. "I'm a good enough one. And no doubt if I got with it or whatever the expression is supposed to be, if I went to your tiresome movies or listened to your ear-insulting so-called music, I'd be a better one. But the price is too high." He stretched out on his lounge chair, yawning. "Let's have some coffee, shall we?" he asked his wife.

Later, in Anne's room, Jimmie lay in bed watching Anne at her dressing table pat her neck and cheeks with brisk fingers. "What are you doing that for?"

"Prevent sagging and wrinkles."

"Aren't you being a bit premature?"

"A woman can never begin too early seeing to her looks. I figure if I start this now I can probably make it to ninety without a crow's foot."

"Do you really care that much about how you're going to look in seventy-six years?" Jimmie thought of her Grandmother Prior's dressing table of beauty aids.

"I certainly do." Anne stopped patting and examined her reflection critically. She curled back her lips and studied her teeth. She picked up a hand mirror and regarded her right profile, and her left. She turned to be able to see how her long shining hair looked from the back.

Jimmie watched this performance with interest, and wondered where the difference—the vast difference—between her and her friend lay. In addition, that was, to her own bewilderingly delayed menstrual onset. Her own eyes were brown and, though innocent of the discreet mascara Anne always wore, were really as nice. Her hair was as

long and as gleamingly well kept. Anne had a better figure—which was to say, Anne *had* a figure, whereas Jimmie herself—

"What *are* you giggling at?" Anne asked.

"Oh, this morning, on the bus—" She stopped. "I don't
know why I laughed. It was awful."

"What was awful?"

"This—creature—was trying to feel my—my bosom, on
the bus this morning, that's all. Except, when I laughed
I was thinking how hard up he must be. Only it isn't
funny. I hate that sort of thing—"

"I suppose," said Anne, climbing into her bed, "it'd depend on who was doing it."

"I don't want anybody doing it."

"Don't you ever think about what it'll be like—making
out? Making *love?*"

"No, I don't."

"Jimmie, you're backward."

"That's what I keep telling you."

"Well, you aren't backward, no matter what you say.
You're just taking your time. Whereas I can't wait. What
do you think about, Jimmie?"

Jimmie was bewildered. What, indeed? She must think.
Only, what about? "I think about books, and school, and
ecology, and Goya." About my parents. I think about
them, and what's wrong with them. "I *think,* that's all.
Don't you ever think about anything but boys and how
you look?"

"Not very often. I guess mainly I think about Dick. I'm
mad about him."

"Oh, Anne."

"No, I mean it. What else is there in life besides love?"

"Do you know what Jane Austen said when they asked
her what she wrote about?"

"What?"

"She said, 'I write of love and money, what else is
there?' "·

"Too right, she was."

"Well, I hope there's something else. I surely hope so.
I hope there's—making it a better world, taking part in
making it better. I hope there's having ideals. That seems
more important to me."

"That's because you've never been in love."

"Anne, you can't be in love with Dick. He's years and years older than you."

"Nine. He's twenty-three. In two years, or at the most three, that won't matter."

"Are you serious?"

"He's all I live for, Jimmie. He's why I wake up in the morning. He's what the day brings me. The sight of him. His voice. Once in a while he looks at me. He's why I hate weekends, because I won't see him. Sometimes I think just being in the same town, being in the same world, with him is enough. But it isn't. I want to see him, be near him." She sighed and lay back, hands behind her head. "Maybe he'll come here and see Pete. Imagine, I never knew they were friends—"

"But he said he was going to Europe, to the British Isles," Jimmie reminded her.

"Don't *talk* about it!" Anne cried out. "I can't face that. I'll die if he goes away." She turned on her side to face Jimmie in the other bed, and in some—to Jimmie frightening—way, her face looked older, and frustrated. "Sometimes, Jimmie, I lie here at night making up stories about him. I pretend that somehow we've got to someplace, in a cabin in a snowstorm maybe if the bus had got lost in a blizzard and we were forced to take shelter together in this cabin by ourselves—"

"Where would the rest of us be, while you were taking shelter? Freezing to death in the bus?"

"Oh, he'd have dropped you all off."

"Why? We aren't the last stop on his route. He'd end up with Faith Powers if he was going to get lost in a blizzard at the end of his run."

"It's my dream," Anne said imperturbably, "and I make it come out the way I want it to. We're in this cabin, by the fire, and he begins, slowly, slowly, to take my clothes off—"

"Stop it," Jimmie said.

Anne laughed, and rolled to her back again. "You're *so* easy to shock, Jimmie."

"I'm not shocked. I just don't think I should share somebody else's erotic—fancies. That's all."

"Okay, okay. But you remember what I say. When love comes, all the rest—ecology, little brothers, big brothers—it all goes out the window."

Well, I don't believe you, Jimmie thought.

But long after Anne had gone to sleep, or into her vision of being disrobed by Dick (for which, incidentally, he'd be thrown in the slammer, Jimmie thought, and wondered if Anne had considered that), Jimmie lay awake, frowning.

I'll get older, she said to herself. Unless I'm a freak or a medical oddity, I'll start having my period and develop a figure and one day want a boy's hands on me. I'll fall in love. But how can everything else go out the window?

She turned on her stomach and thought about Peter and his father, talking together. They disagreed about so many things, but there was always the underlying effort to reach each other, understand each other. She thought about dinner conversations at her own house, the war of words that went on between her mother and father and made her own stomach rebel at food.

Last night her father had been talking about mankind's history of war-making, and how progress had been made in man's thinking. "All things considered," he'd said, "we've really made *some* progress in getting world opinion to turn against war as a solution to population to economic stresses."

"All things considered," Mrs. Gavin had said, carefully cutting the fat from her pork chop, then putting a delicate bite in her mouth and chewing, swallowing, before she went on, not looking up, "all things considered, mankind has not made progress in any direction whatsoever. In a world where atom bombs have been dropped and napalm is manufactured for profit in one country to be dropped upon the people of another country in the name of bringing it peace and the franchise, no progress of any kind can be said to have been made."

"Don't put me in the position of defending any war. I just said that there seems to be some sort of enlightenment in human beings as to just what war actually does to people."

"You sound like that terrible writer, whose name I can't bring myself to pronounce, who talked about the ultimate triumph of the human spirit but admitted he'd go into the streets of Mississippi with a gun to defend its rights as a state—and we all know what that means. Nobel prize winner he was. Another man who believed in the remedial power of the gun."

"Why do you keep trying to push me into the role of militant?"

"I'm not trying to push you anywhere. I'm just saying what I think man*kind* is like. There are some processes that are not reversible, and the ultimate decay of the human spirit is one."

"If you really believe that, why are you living at all?"

"Good question."

By now they were staring into each other's eyes, food forgotten, children forgotten.

"Mankind, you say," Dr. Gavin had gone on. "Would womankind have done better?"

His wife lifted slender shoulders, let them fall. "I hold no brief for women. Except that I think they'd go at things differently. A woman would *know* what the dropped napalm was going to do to people—the agony of it— the children who'd be seared. The innocents and the guilty—whoever the guilty are—*but* in agony. I don't think a woman would drop a bomb, or shove a bayonet into another human being."

"If you were in a battle situation, you'd think differently. When it's your life or the other fellow's, you save your own."

"I'd never be in a battle situation."

"Of course you wouldn't. That's why you can't understand what you're talking about."

"I mean, if I were a *man,* I wouldn't be in a battle situation. I'd be in Canada or Sweden or in jail, but not in a jungle where it was my life or the other fellow's."

"All right," said Dr. Gavin, leaning forward. "All right —then let me put it this way. Suppose you were on a city street and someone aimed a gun at you, meaning to use it. Wouldn't you shoot first, if you could?"

"How could I shoot first? I wouldn't have a gun."

"I'd have given you one," he said. "For self-defense on the perilous streets of New York."

"But I wouldn't take it."

Jimmie, swallowing hard, thought to herself that in a way this should be sort of funny. And it wasn't funny at all. She'd glanced at Goya, hoping for one of his irrelevant interruptions, but he, elbows on the table, chin on his fists, was all but asleep.

Before Jimmie could think of a distraction to offer, Mrs. Gavin went on, "I wouldn't carry a gun, so there'd be no point in your having offered it to me."

"I'd have begged you to carry it. For the sake of your husband and your children. So, now you've got a gun and the mugger or rapist, or whatever he is, is aiming at you. What do you do?"

"I let him shoot."

"The hell you do."

"Well, I do. I ought to know what I'd do."

"That's just my point. You don't know what you'd do."

"This is an asinine conversation." Mrs. Gavin had pushed her chair away from the table. "Jimmie, help me clear, please."

"Hold on a second." Dr. Gavin had raised his hand, and his wife and daughter sat on the edge of their chairs. "Let me put it this way—"

"You sound like Nixon," Mrs. Gavin muttered.

"Never mind what I sound like—"

"I'd mind if I sounded like that—"

"Will you let me finish!" he yelled.

"Please do."

"You've got this gun—"

"So you say."

"Okay, so I say. I say you've got this gun, and the guy is aiming not at you, but at Jimmie or Goya. And the *only* way for you to save them is to *shoot to kill.* What then?"

"I should have known," she said softly. "I should have known that's what you'd do. Lead me into a semantic sentimental cliché trap. Well, if it gives you satisfaction to have me admit that given all your hypotheses, I'd kill a human being—all right, I'd kill him." She stood up. "Will you please finish serving dinner to your father and Goya, Jimmie. I'm going upstairs."

There were families where people could sit at dinner talking of abstract things, beautiful things, terrible things, without turning every discussion into a contest where blood was meant to be drawn.

Finally getting sleepy, Jimmie relaxed, wiped away a tear she hadn't realized was gathering, and thought that of course there were such families. Maybe lots of them. She just didn't happen to belong to one, that was all.

CHAPTER TEN

On a Saturday morning in late March, icy, easterly, and gray, Mrs. Gavin appeared for breakfast wearing a look of assault that Jimmie knew from experience meant they were about to do some housecleaning. Her mother had these sporadic attacks when she damned the house as a pigsty and threatened to clean it from attic to cellar. Generally by the time a crumb-caked toaster, a grease-limed waffle iron, and some kitchen shelves had been burnished and scrubbed, the wave of purification passed and Mrs. Gavin retreated to her room, exhausted and satisfied.

Jimmie rather enjoyed these times, when her mother, sitting back on her heels and thoughtfully regarding a closet, would say things like, "Zelda Fitzgerald claimed that pots and pans breed under the kitchen sink. And see, she was right. Ours have reproduced."

"Morning, Beth," said Dr. Gavin. "Did you sleep well?"

Why does he always *ask* her that, Jimmie thought irritably. She tried to remember the last time her father had said, "Good morning, darling," to his wife. Had he called her darling or cared to hear her answer to anything lately?

"I was up till all hours, rereading *Jude the Obscure*: The television program is so good, I wanted to compare. What a peculiar man that Hardy was. He really loved strong-minded, independent women, with a streak of wild-

90

ness in them, but he always punished them so brutally for being what he'd made them, what he admired." As she spoke, Mrs. Gavin had poured herself a cup of coffee and put a piece of bread in the toaster. She sat down, and Dr. Gavin lowered his newspaper a little to acknowledge her presence at the table. "Actually," she went on, "I suppose it was really Victoria's influence that made him so harsh on unconventional women. That wretched little queen did more to demean and debase the lot of her sex than most men ever did."

Dr. Gavin didn't comment. Jimmie lifted her long hair away from her shoulders and let it fall. "What're we going to clean today, Mom?"

"How did you know we were going to clean anything?"

"You have that cleaning gleam in your eye."

Mrs. Gavin smiled and picked up the front section of the *Times,* her husband having already got to the second section and the sports news. "I thought we'd get the summer clothes out of the bedroom closets and into the attic storage space."

Jimmie laughed with real amusement, and at her mother's quirked brow, said, "Mother, it's already March. The summer dresses and the cotton slacks have been cohabiting with jersey jumpers and woolen pants for the better part of the winter. Why separate them now?"

"Well, I just thought—" Mrs. Gavin broke off, frowning. "This latest war criminal we've tried—" she began, and Dr. Gavin gripped his newspaper convulsively, while Jimmie fought to restrain a sigh. "I suppose," Mrs. Gavin went on, not noticing them, "that now that he's a convicted murderer we'll make an American folk hero out of him, the way we did that little thug, Billy the Kid."

Dr. Gavin put his paper down. "Have you anything, ever, that's good to say about this country?"

"I imagine if I thought for a minute I might have."

"While you're thinking, let me pose you a question. Has there ever been any other country where a huge portion of its citizens rose up to try to prevent its government from continuing a war?"

"Perhaps not. Of course, there have never been other wars like this one. Nothing can justify a war, but in most there's been some semblance of ideology, distorted though it might have been. You're trying to retain your colonies, or protect your shores, or avenge yourself for wrongs perpetrated upon you at the conclusion of an earlier war. In Vietnam, and Korea—I think I'll add the Mexican-American War—it has been simply and solely the exercise and pursuit of power on the part of the military, backed by reactionary and stupid and insensitive administrations—"

"Watch out, now," said Dr. Gavin. "You're backing into a Democratic Administration, with the Korean War on your plate."

"Truman was a stupid, insensitive, reactionary man. And these wars have been the brute aggression of a strong nation upon weak and defenseless ones. There's no other way to look at them."

"I wish I were as sure of myself once in a while as you are of yourself all the time."

"There may be an answer to that, but offhand I can't think of it."

"If you're so unalterably opposed to your country's policies, why are you still in it?"

She shrugged. "I don't think there's anyplace better, or not much better, to go to. And some are worse. At least we still *can* mount an anti-war movement—"

"You've noticed that?"

"Yes. They bring in the National Guard with tear gas and guns to disperse such movements, killing off a few kids in the process, of course. But yes, we can still have them, for all the effect they've had—which is none."

"It was the Peace Movement got Mr. Johnson out of office."

"And only see what we got instead. But anyway, as to your question, even if there were some other country I thought I could live in, my family is here. I think people are more important than places."

"Do you? You know something—I am absolutely sick to death of the pound, pound, pound of your social and political conscience upon the body of our family. Especially, I'll add, since it is all talk and no works. Who are you to talk about peace parades? The farthest you ever get from home is the Massic River branch library. And don't," he said, raising his voice, "tell me you go to your mother's every year, because that isn't *going* someplace, as far as I'm concerned, it's *returning*. Can't you see at all that I need a rest from Vietnam, and Cambodia, and the Administration. I want to find some pleasure in life. I don't *want* to suffer over the world's wrongs every bloody minute. There've been wars since the first goddam slugs crawled out of the slime, probably, and there will be until the planet is blown up, which you're right in saying probably will be—"

"How do you stay so thin?" Faith Powers had wailed one day to Jimmie.

A steady diet of dissension at the table, Jimmie felt like saying. That'll keep the kilos off. She said, "I kicked the chocolate habit," and thought of adding, "Now I live mainly on Rolaids," but, of course, did not.

CHAPTER ELEVEN

On an afternoon in April, Jimmie sat on the window seat in her room looking out at a mixture of snow and rain falling from a rough sky and blowing across the back yard and garden. She told herself it was spring.

"The raccoons are back!" Goya had shouted at her that morning.

"How do you know?"

"Because the driveway is covered with garbage," he'd shouted joyfully.

The robins were back.

Spring.

The thick wet falling mixture blackened boughs and trunks of leafless trees and turned a line of crocuses that yesterday had looked sturdy as little lamps into sleazy-petaled failures. There were some tentative green shoots on the skinny, tangled branches of a huge forsythia bush that grew beside the garage and later on would bloom butter-yellow and dazzling to the eye. Now it looked unkempt and trashy, something only chickadees and titmice, sheltering in its wreathing branches, could love.

Just outside Jimmie's window was a tiny balcony, scarcely to be called that, where on summer nights she sometimes sat on a cushion, knees hugged to her chest, listening to the sounds of insects in the grass, of television in neighboring houses, of traffic going past at the front of the house. Listening, she would tell herself, to her thoughts.

But at this time of year, even though the calendar said spring, it was difficult to imagine opening the window, far less sitting out there on the balcony in the night air. She had, a few years before, attached a bird-feeder to the balcony railing and all winter long chickadees and tit-mice, blue jays and cardinals, came to share at her board. She provided them with the best. Sunflower seed. Chicka-dees and titmice and nuthatches would flash across from the dogwood tree or the lilac bush or the hemlock, to take a seed and fly back to where they'd started from, with a friendly sort of openness, almost as if they knew this feast was not accidental, but offered to them. Cardi-nals were furtive. They took a long time making up their minds to approach the feeder at all, and when they did, would grab and make a getaway like burglars. Mostly they preferred picking off the ground what the other birds spilled from the feeder. Blue jays, more often than not, simply sat on the railing, husking seeds with rapid movements of their bills, not, like the smaller birds, hold-ing the seed down with their feet to beat the kernel out against a twig.

By winter's end there was always a huge area of sun-flower-seed husks beneath Jimmie's window and each year her father said it'd be a miracle if any grass grew there at all. "We'll have this big bald spot on our lawn," he'd predict, but each year the miracle occurred and somehow the husks of the birds' winter victualing disappeared into the ground and the grass arose. But even if the grass hadn't grown, Dr. Gavin admitted, these small creatures, by their bright unfailing presence all year long, more than earned their little keep. Jimmie had wanted to keep the feeder filled in summer, too, to attract migrants—thrushes and catbirds and towhees and thrashers and maybe even orioles—but Dr. Gavin had said it would give the fledg-lings impractical ideas about just what it was they were supposed to eat and where they were supposed to get it.

"And look at it this way," he'd pointed out to Jimmie. "Suppose we moved away and the next people didn't both-er to fill the feeder, then there's a chance, if we left at just that time of year that the fledglings are fledging, that they'd simply starve because they'd got it in their heads that dinner comes on a wooden tray and not out there in the trees."

"Why should we move?" Jimmie had asked, fastening on what, at the moment, seemed to her the most alarming part of his exposition.

She couldn't recall, now, if he'd answered.

What an awful, what a dreary late-winter rainy snow this was. Goya's footsteps, crossing the driveway and yard to the hedge separating him from Kenny next door, were black traceries in the slush. People were always quoting the poet who'd called April the cruelest month, and they had reason, even if they didn't know which poet it was. Cruel, wet, without end, that was April.

What Jimmie waited for, each year, was the first appearance of the red-winged blackbirds. Their glossy black, scarlet-slashed forms were like an announcement. "You may not believe this, but Spring is just behind us, right on our tail feathers." And then she waited for the night when, as if they had never left, the peepers returned with their piping. The sweetest, the dearest sound in the world, she sometimes thought—that of the spring peepers in the dark. They sound like tiny birds, don't they? Well, they aren't. They're tiny frogs.

She turned her attention from the yard and the feeder —where a couple of wet, rumple-feathered sparrows were quarreling, although there was plenty of seed for both—and looked around this room of hers that she thought so much nicer than the rooms of any of her friends. Even Marcy's, so much bigger and more handsomely furnished, didn't have the charming sass of this one. Or anyway, that's how it seems to me, thought Jimmie, who tended to qualify nearly everything she said or thought.

There were her shelves full of books, of little china figures from Beatrix Potter stories, of uninteresting shells and stones from Jones Beach, and interesting ones from the gift shop at the Museum of Natural History. There was a branch of rosy coral from a Caribbean reef, brought back by one of Dr. Gavin's patients, Mrs. Israel, who had also brought to Goya a large piece of sponge, and had told him it was a living thing.

"A simple, multicellular sessile organism," she'd said to Goya in the office that day, and Goya's mouth had opened in amazement—not at the words, although Jimmie, and Mrs. Israel, knew he liked to be addressed in polysyllables—but at the idea that this tan bouncy ball of holes in his hand was alive, and no one had quite got around to explaining that it had been once but no longer was.

"What's sessile?" Jimmie had asked.

"A sessile creature is one that is permanently fixed. It cannot get around but must take its nourishment and for all I know of that, its entertainment, too, in the place where it lives."

Like my mother, Jimmie had thought.

"What does it do for entertainment?"

Mrs. Israel's eyes had twinkled. "Oh, observes the passing parade, I should think. Probably pretty interesting down there in the ocean. Marvelous fish, old pirate vessels, treasure—who *knows* what."

Goya, from all this, had plucked one salient fact. His sponge was a living thing.

In the afternoon—it had been on a hot summer day that the gifts from the Caribbean were presented—he had asked Jimmie to take him to the park. There, in the barely flowing, thoroughly polluted narrow brown river that gave their town its name, he set his sponge at liberty.

"Why are you taking that with you?" Jimmie had asked, steering her bicycle carefully, with Goya on the bar in front. "Goya, I said why do you have the sponge with you?"

She'd thought perhaps he meant to surprise her by washing the bike, and was trying to figure how to tell him she'd rather have it washed in water from the hose at home, not in the filthy Massic River.

Goya, who sometimes answered people and sometimes did not, this time did not.

When they got to the river bank, he stooped down somberly, patted his sponge on its back (or that part of it, Jimmie decided, that he had decided was its back) then gently tipped it into the sluggishly moving river, where it floated against a fallen log and seemed to have lost its freedom before beginning to find it. Jimmie, who by now had got the drift of her brother's thinking, debated with herself only briefly about telling him the facts of life and death from the sponge's point of view, and then with a sigh realized that for Goya, this sponge, along with Santa Claus and the Tooth Fairy, was going to live.

She leaned over and lifted it clear of the log, and they watched as, revolving like Eeyore, it made its slow way down the river and out of their lives.

But not out of our minds, Jimmie thought now, smiling. Never will that sponge be erased from our minds.

Her room had been furnished by Grandmother Prior with things from the Prior house in upstate Connecticut. Caramel-colored wood, chintz coverings, rag rugs. In a corner of the room was her old doll house, built by her father, with the little family arrested in the poses in which she'd abandoned them years before. Like the little toy soldier and the little toy dog, they were covered with dust and awaiting the touch of a vanished hand and the sound of a voice that was still. Except, of course, that her hand and voice were still active—only not for the doll-house family any more. Once in a while she considered storing it in the attic, but the right time to do it never came. It was always either summer, when the attic would be oven-hot and probably wasp-ridden, or it was winter and the attic would be freezing. In the spring and the fall she never remembered, which probably meant she didn't wish to. So the doll house remained in its corner, never touched, never dusted, almost never looked at. Just there. And the wall across from her bed, the wall with the door in it, was something she thought one day she'd do something about, too. But the longer she left it as it was, crayoned, penciled, painted, covered with graffiti, with telephone numbers, with sketches and still lifes and portraits contributed by friends and relations, the less it seemed possible to paint it over.

It was six or seven years now since her father, painting the room, had handed her a box of acrylics and said, "While I'm working on these walls, Jimmie, why don't you paint a mural on that one?"

"A mural?"

"Any wall painting is a mural. Paint something."

"On the *wall?*"

"Yes."

"What should I paint?" she asked, thrilled.

"Anything you want. The whole wall's yours."

Tongue in the corner of her mouth, at first making little nervous strokes, but quickly emboldened, she had
painted the story of Hansel and Gretel from the door-
jamb to the corner where her wall met one of her father's. Hansel and Gretel and the witch and the gingerbread house and some spiky flowers still trailed along
near the baseboard. Above them, during the years, had
burgeoned and blossomed and spread paintings and mark-
ings and diagrams and maps and messages until the wall
was covered to the ceiling. Anne, who couldn't draw anything but the rear view of a rabbit, had drawn hundreds
of them. Marcy had painted birds and flowers that Mrs.
Gavin said could have come from an illuminated manu-
script. Chris Martin had painted a nude male figure that
Dr. Gavin said looked like some frescoes at Pompeii that
women weren't allowed to see. They'd painted him out
and put a tree in his place. "Because of my grandmothers,"
Jimmie had told Chris. "They'd be shocked." But the
truth was, she herself hadn't liked that boy sticking out
that way on her wall.

Like the doll house, the wall seemed to have remained
in her room but not in her life. She looked at it now,
trying to remember the last time anyone had added anything. Ages ago. She couldn't remember when. Yet she
didn't think she wanted it painted over. It was part of
things, part of the past, part of friendships and nonsense,
part of her father's funny and wayward humor that she
saw in him less and less.

Sometimes, when her father came in late in the day, he
liked to have something hot to drink. Especially on raw
bleak days in winter and spring. This afternoon, when
he'd come home, Mrs. Gavin had asked, "Would you
like something to drink?"

"That'd be fine."

"Tea or coffee?"

"Well—tea, if you have it," he'd answered.

"Why do you *always* say that? Would I offer you tea if I didn't have it? Do you think I specialize in minor versions of malicious mischief?"

"Forget it," Dr. Gavin had said, starting up the stairs. "I don't want anything."

Jimmie had gone into her room without waiting to see her father. She'd been sitting on the window seat ever since.

What kind of a conversation was that? If you repeated it to someone, it wouldn't sound as if a quarrel had taken place. But it didn't, either, sound like a chat between friends or acquaintances. It had to be the sort of exchange that took place in a family, because people just weren't that biting with friends—or acquaintances. Or strangers. It was a shame that families didn't treat one another like strangers. If they did, maybe there'd be better manners and less unkindness.

And now here came Goya, thrusting through the hedge, stumping across the driveway and lawn to the back door, black squashy boot patterns oozing up behind him like monster prints in a movie. Bang of the door, a longish pause that said he had remembered, or been reminded, to take his boots off, then sounds of Goya stamping upstairs.

Her door was flung open. No knock. It didn't seem the time to bring that to his attention.

"Kenny and I had this fight."

"What about, this time?"

"About if he could push me down the stairs."

"Oh, for goodness sakes. Why did he want to push you down the stairs?"

"He didn't *want* to. He did." Goya thought that over. "I guess he wanted to, too."

"You mean—down the stairs? From *up*stairs? All the way down? He actually *did* that?"

"Yup."

Jimmie was outraged. "Are you hurt?"

"Nope."

"I'm going over and see his mother."

Goya shook his head. "No. Anyway, she already knows he did it. She smacked him and told him to go stay in his room. And she told me to go home and don't come back until we can get along."

"Goya—why don't you go to see one of your other friends? One you don't have fights with. Why is it always Kenny?"

"He's the closest."

"Oh boy. You and that kid can't be together ten minutes without getting into a fight. I should think you'd hate each other."

"I should think so, too," Goya agreed, but it was apparent that he didn't in the least hate Kenny. "So I decided," he went on, "to come play with you instead. Less you and me play Scrabble."

His legs were plump and sturdy, his cheeks whipped pink by the wet April air, and he sparkled with good humor, with lack of animus at Kenny, with anticipation of playing with Jimmie.

"He is so like his father, when his father was that age," Gram had said, "that sometimes when I look at him, or listen to him, I seem to be lost in time. Or in memory, I suppose."

And her father still, in many ways, shared Goya's high-hearted bearing, his air of expecting marvels, of having, indeed, already encountered marvels. Even now, although her parents tangled with each other like Goya and Kenny —on a higher? anyway, on a bitterer level—her father's reaction, once he'd removed himself from the scene of contention, was to brighten, to laugh about something, to forget that he had, so to speak, just been pushed down the stairs. Like Goya, thought Jimmie, he goes off and plays with someone else.

She frowned, forming this picture, because she thought she'd been referring to herself and all at once was not so sure. Was her father playing games with somebody else?

Once, recently, her mother, standing at the living-room window looking out at the night, at the moon, had said, "How strange it must be, to have an astronaut for a husband. To be down here, looking up there, knowing that right now, at this very second, your husband is walking over the moon's crust."

Grandmother Prior, who'd been paying a weekend visit, had said with a short sniff, "At least *they* know where their husbands are."

Mrs. Gavin had walked out of the room and hadn't

come down again that evening. When her father got in, Jimmie said to him casually, "We missed you at dinner. It was lamb, the way you like it."

"Sorry I missed it." Then, as she was clearly waiting, he added, "I was with a salesman from a dental supply company. I'm going to get one of those jazzy new chairs that glide up and down and look good enough for Madame Récamier to pose in."

"Oh. That's nice."

He'd got the new dental chair. Practically a lounge, that with a touch of his foot would silently bring his patient floating up to the drill, or send him down near the floor and freedom. Covered in aqua green vinyl. Jazzy.

"Jimmie?"

"Yes, Goya?"

"Aren't we going to play?"

"I'll tell you—let's go see what Daddy's doing. He came home a while ago, and I bet he's working on his chess set."

CHAPTER TWELVE

Chris Martin lived with her mother and her mother's second husband, Mr. Charles Duclair, and three stepsisters, in a big rhododendron-ringed brown clapboard house in a better part of town than the Gavins lived in. When Jimmie had first heard the name, Charles Duclair, she had pictured someone elegant, accented, probably associated with the United Nations.

Not a bit of it. Mr. Duclair had turned out to be a florid, successful-salesman type, with a lot of flab and the sort of self-pitying look of a man living with five women who had long since taken the reins from his hands, if he'd ever held them.

Jimmie hadn't wanted, especially, to go to Chris's slumber party. It wasn't because she didn't like Chris, she liked her very much, and thought it would be fun to spend a night with her and Anne and Marcy. But she was unaccustomed to visiting, except now and then at Anne's. Practically no one came to her house overnight. Her mother said she was not up to invasions of teenagers. Jimmie felt funny about accepting invitations because of this.

But Anne had talked her into it. "Friendship isn't *bookkeeping*, you know. Besides, it won't be as much fun for us if you aren't there."

Such a direct compliment quite won Jimmie over, and she felt happy as she and Anne rode a city bus on this mild May afternoon toward Chris's party.

But she wondered, as they rode along, if she shared some of her mother's detachment from people, her lack of curiosity about even those closest to her. The condition of humanity was her mother's great concern, but she didn't care for close-up relationships. Jimmie recalled a phrase from Tom Paine, read during her American History course—*He pities the plumage, but forgets the dying bird.* He'd been talking about people like her mother, people so passionately solicitous about humanity that they lost sight of human beings.

She thought about Anne, who was into everyone's business, who was a well—practically a geyser—of sympathy. Who was observant. Anne would notice when a teacher appeared in a new dress or hairdo. If you'd had some sort of worry on Friday, she'd remember to ask you about it on Monday. She'd gone across town to the hospital to visit Bunny when he was laid up that time, taking him candy and a couple of paperback mysteries. She managed to do all this, get acceptable grades, be as vain and self-involved as anyone Jimmie had ever known, and all at the same time.

For instance, only yesterday Anne had asked Faith Powers if she'd had a good time in Bermuda. Jimmie had forgotten about Faith's Easter vacation plans, and if she'd remembered wouldn't have asked about them, for fear Faith might reply at too great length. Anne, on the other hand, had sat all during lunch listening to Faith's description of a five-day gala not one word of which could be believed. If she isn't lying, Jimmie had thought, leaving halfway through the recital, then her parents ought to be in an institution.

She said now, "Did you really believe any of that stuff Faith was telling you yesterday about her blast in Bermuda?"

"Oh, no. Poor Faith."

"Then why do you encourage her to talk that way? I think it's cynical of you."

"Oh, Jimmie—some things I am, but cynical I'm not. No, I just think the poor thing has to have somebody to talk to sometimes. I know she's lying, and she knows she's lying, and she knows I know, too. But if it makes her feel better, where's the harm?"

"There's always harm in lying," Jimmie said, not sure she could have defended the statement if Anne had taken her up on it. She set herself now the charge of asking something personal and important about Anne, to show them both that she, too, could be observant and concerned. Since they were on a bus, the obvious question was about Dick Mosher. Come to think of it, Anne hadn't talked about him in ages, or doted upon him, her wide blue eyes fixed on the back of his head as they rode to school. The last time she'd spoken of him was a few weeks back, when she'd telephoned after school to ask Jimmie if she'd noticed, now that Dick had shed his big jacket, how his shoulder muscles moved under the Irish sweater he'd taken to wearing. Jimmie hadn't observed this, but Anne said the sight of him made the backs of her knees and the insides of her elbows tingle.

"How's your—uh—your—ah—"

Anne, turning her head a little, smiled and waited.

"I mean to say—I was wondering how you feel about Dick these days. If you're still—oh, well—"

"Jimmie Gavin, are you *afraid* to use the word love?"

"I'm not afraid to use it. I just don't like using it where I don't think it has—has any place."

"You really do believe a person has to be a certain age before she can fall in love, don't you? Like getting a driver's license, or into an X-rated movie."

Jimmie moved uncomfortably. That was precisely what she believed, but Anne made it sound retarded. "I suppose you can have a crush," she conceded.

"Well, actually you're so right. *But, after all, my erstwhile dear, my no longer cherished—need we say it was not love, just because it perished?*"

Jimmie had to laugh. "Did you make that up?" she asked admiringly.

"Of course not. You flatter me. It's Edna Millay, one of those romantic writers not in your books." She sighed. "I guess it was a crush, all right, but it was delicious while it lasted. Now I have nobody to think about before I go to sleep and nobody to wake *up* for. Except boys I invent in my head, of course. Life seems terribly *empty*," she said, her light clear voice so vivacious that a couple of passengers turned to smile at her.

"How did you recover?" Jimmie asked curiously. "Wasn't it sort of sudden?"

"Not really. He and Peter have become sort of friendly, when Dick had *time* for friendship, which isn't often because he works all the time. The first time he came to the house, I almost swooned. I mean, I really thought that rapture would overcome me and I'd lose consciousness, but I just fell into a chair instead and gazed my fill upon him. But I'll tell you something funny," she continued in a serious tone. "You can't go on loving someone who doesn't love you back. Who doesn't seem to *notice* you, practically. Anyway, I can't. You read about unrequited love and its staying power, and it's practically the *foundation* of drama, but it doesn't *work*, even if you want it to. I was reading this book Mother brought home, *Birds of America*, by Mary McCarthy—I was thinking maybe I'd lend it to you, because you're so crazy about birds and all, but it isn't about that. Birds. It's about people, and she's terribly wordy, so I just skimmed, but she has this place in it where she says there's no such thing as unreciprocated love, and I thought at first, Oh *joy*—if she's right, and Mother says she's one of the brightest women in the world so chances are she would be, then Dick will just *have* to love me because I can't go unre*cip*rocated, but really what she must have meant was nobody can keep *on* loving if they aren't reciprocated, not just that because you love somebody they have to love you back, don't you think?"

Squirming under so many repetitions of the word love, Jimmie felt like saying, What I think is that you've just delivered a thousand-word paragraph with no punctuation in it. And yet she was glad to be here with Anne, on their way to Chris Martin's slumber party, to be in the company of a group of girls who would play music and stay up late and probably talk about love and boys most of the time.

Backward, all right, she thought. But trying to catch up.

Chris's house could easily have accommodated, in separate rooms, the four girls who were to make up the party, in addition to Chris's stepsister, Sally, who was going to be their chaperone. But they were bringing sleeping bags, and planned, all of them except Sally, to doss down in Chris's room. Anne's sleeping bag was flowery, fluffy, and filled with down. Jimmie had an ancient one that had belonged to her father when he'd been a Boy Scout. She figured it was stuffed with pinfeathers and wouldn't have parted with it for the best that Abercrombie carried.

"What we'll do," said Chris, greeting them with a whoop of delight, "is we'll stash the bags in my room and if we ever decide to go to sleep we can spread out up there. Marcy's here already. She's in the kitchen with my mother and Sally. The other two wicked stepsisters are out of town. Come on, we'll get the hellos over and pry Marcy loose, and then we can go upstairs and play some music until the oldsters leave. I've wired up this quadrophonic system, did I tell you, and attached four colored footlights to it so they flash and flutter with the beat. I've really about decided to be an engineer—"

Marcy, sitting on a bar-stool at the kitchen table, shoulders curved forward, looked up at their entrance with a fleeting smile. She was peeling potatoes. She always, wherever she went, tried to find something to do that would allow her to sit down, but seemed uneasy on the high stool and more stooped even than usual.

Why doesn't she straighten up? Jimmie thought. Why don't her parents, her doctor, why doesn't *somebody*, give her the confidence to put her shoulders back? She could be positively regal, she could be a beauty, and she goes through life hunched over like Quasimodo. And maybe, if the time ever comes when she realizes what she *could* be, how she *should* stand, it'll be too late. She'll be permanently curved, like a birch tree.

I wonder why we don't tell people things for their own good, if they really are for their own good, if we really care for them? She supposed that her father would answer to that, that you don't tell anybody anything. People learn or find out, sometimes, what's good for them, what their way should be, but learn from inside, not from well-intentioned directions from teachers or relatives or friends. He'd said that, or something like enough, one time when she'd asked why he didn't *tell* Mother to be cheerful, to find some joy somewhere in life.

"She could *assume* a virtue, if she has it not," she'd quoted (or misquoted) to her father. "Because joy in life is a virtue, isn't it, even if so much in the world is wrong?"

"Husbands," he had said in a remote voice, "are supposed to bring joy to their wives. I appear to be a failure in that department."

"Oh, it isn't *your* fault, I didn't mean *that*," she'd said, reproaching herself for not seeing how he'd take her words, how he was obliged to take them. "I just mean—Mother sort of *stares* into the gloomiest corner. I thought maybe we could suggest she try—oh, looking out the window."

"You certainly have a way with a metaphor, Jimmie. But some people prefer looking in corners."

Did Marcy prefer to slink through life curved and tentative as a question mark?

Sally Duclair was sixteen and went to a private school where Chris also could have gone, Mr. Duclair saying he'd certainly not favor his own three girls over his wife's one. But Chris had refused, telling her friends that she didn't see much point in getting started at a place she'd probably have to leave in a couple of years, which was what she gave her mother's present marriage. She said things like this quite openly, and Jimmie didn't see how they could fail to get back to Mr. and Mrs. Duclair, but they apparently didn't hear what she said or didn't care what she said. The Duclairs, from what little Jimmie knew of them, didn't care about anything but parties and drinking. She knew, from Chris, that they were going out tonight to some bash across town and wouldn't get back until all hours and when they did would be too drunk to notice if the slumber party had been attacked and dismembered. If Jimmie's mother, or Anne's or Marcy's, had known that this overnight was to be chaperoned by a sixteen year old who looked twenty but on an IQ test wouldn't have had trouble passing for twelve, none of them would have got to go. ("Does she look sixteen when she takes all that make-up off?" Jimmie had asked

Chris, who'd said, "God no, then she looks thirty.") However, the Beggses, the Ferrises, the Gavins and the Duclairs had nothing in common but their daughters, and apparently nobody had thought to inquire about something their daughters were not about to disclose.

So, here we are, thought Jimmie, listening to Mrs. Duclair outline what they were to have for dinner. Steak, which they'd be able to do outdoors on the grill because it was such a nice night. French fries, for which Marcy was fixing the potatoes. Salad. "And make something or other for dessert, if you want. There's dozens of mixes in the pantry, and ice cream, and—" Mrs. Duclair didn't bother to finish the inventory. "I'm going up and dress now, girls. Ta-ta." As she talked, she'd been sipping from a short glass of water-colored liquid that nobody thought was water, and now she polished it off and licked her lips.

Except, Jimmie thought, she really doesn't have any lips. Just a mouth and a frozen little smile. She had thin arms and legs and a protuberant stomach. She wore beautiful clothes.

In another half hour she and her husband were gone. To a cocktail party at one place, Chris said, and on to a dinner party somewhere else. "The usual weekend routine. And the way they drive! Duclair was stopped by the fuzz last Saturday, and he couldn't even get out of the car, much less pass a balloon test. And did they do anything to him? They did not. He knows every politician in town, and the cops know he does, so they just let him bomb on home. If he'd been a kid, or a black, or from the west end of town, he'd have been in leg-irons for a month. But not Chas Duclair. And he *told* all about it the next day. He gets his ego-massage from that kind of thing. The way he drives, somebody's going to be killed one day. Chas himself, if Justice is on the *qui vive.* Or would you say, on the *qui morte?*"

Sally Duclair, as if Chris hadn't spoken at all, said, "You kids want to make a cake, or just have ice cream and cookies?"

After dinner they sat on lawn chairs on the grass in the gathering dark, Jimmie trying to hear the peepers through their voices, through the music blasting out of Chris's second-story back window. Chris had put on tapes of Janis Joplin, Jimi Hendrix, the Beatles—those performers beloved by a generation ahead of them and now dead or dispersed but still throbbing with pain or a kind of stabbing hilarity. The peepers, steady and compulsive and indifferent to human sounds, somehow made themselves heard, and that was a comfort.

I'm not really a groupy type, Jimmie thought. I don't like noise enough, or talking.

She looked around at this company of which she was, in fact, a part. How comfortable, protected, suburban we look. Happy people with happy problems, as the fellow said. The Martian eye, regarding us, would say to itself—in the old Martian talking-eye style—*"There's* a top-drawer selection of humanoids."

Yet they weren't, the four of them, really of the top drawer in high school, not of the In group, that special caste to be found in any high school or college or country club or ghetto . . . the *in* Ins, who glitter when they walk.

And it—belonging to that caste—wasn't primarily a matter of how much money your family had. Marcy was the richest girl in school. In fact, it was the Beggs Senior High School that they went to. Marcy would one day be a debutante. Not that she wanted to be. The whole process would be agony to her shy, unpretentious spirit, but it was Mrs. Beggs, not Marcy, who decided most of Marcy's actions. And Mr. Beggs, once a year at commencement exercises, stood up like the pillar of community life he certainly was—a tall, sinewy, take-charge type with modish sideburns and discreetly mod dress—and said he *believed* in the fine public school system of their town. "All my children, and my grandchildren, too, if *I* have anything to say about it (murmur of polite laughter from the audience) will receive their educations here in these halls and classrooms, and a finer education they could not find anywhere, why in a recent national poll our school system placed—" Etc., etc., etc.

"Does your friend Marcy have brothers?" Dr. Gavin had asked Jimmie one day.

"No. She's an only. Why?"

"I was just wondering, if her father did have sons whether he'd have beaten them into shape, too. Or out of it. Like Marcy. I sort of liked the notion that he might be nursing a revolutionary in his bosom. On the other hand, the revolutionary wouldn't be in his bosom, would he? He's the sort of authoritarian, buy-American, fight-American father figure who throws a dissenting son out of his house and his life and his affections."

"How do you know? Not that I don't agree."

"Heard him at that town meeting I went to, the one about the anti-pollution drive for the Massic. He's all against pollution, of course, and don't get him wrong, but on the other hand The Beggs Chemical Company, Inc., provides employment for many Massic River residents and there are no quick and easy solutions for where to dump chemical wastes no matter what the environmentalists with their scare tactics would have you believe. He waxed pretty passionate over 'so-called ecologists and crazy kids with their conservation fads' who are trying to block the progress of the country, meaning industry, meaning especially The Beggs Chemical Company, Inc. You know, he somehow contrived to include the Atomic Energy Commission, which is being hampered in its patriotic attempts to test missiles by 'commies and do-gooders' who care more about animals and trees than they do about the people, who need *power*. Atomic power, he was talking about, not power to the people. Quite a speech, all in all. I'm glad your mother wasn't there."

"Did *any*one talk against him?"

"One fellow got up and sort of nervously suggested that the people need clean water and wilderness and some sort of natural heritage to leave for future generations—a place safe from industrial depredations, he said. He wasn't forceful, and didn't actually *name*, by name, The Beggs Chemical Company, Inc., as an industrial depredator which is dumping into the Massic in the interests of the people. Maybe the fellow was a real hero, though, and is employed by Beggs. Was employed, would be the operative term, no doubt, if that's the case."

"Did you say something, Daddy?"

"Honey, sorry to let you down, but I'm not a fit adversary for Mr. Beggs. I'm not up to public debate with a human rhinoceros like your friend's father."

Marcy, despite her father's money and power, was not an In person, probably because of her terrible, terrifying shyness. With Anne and Jimmie, with Chris to some extent, even though Chris sometimes seemed like a one-girl invasion of her friends' inner beings, Marcy felt unthreatened. Felt loved.

And as to money—Chris's pro tem father had barrels of bread. But Chris was too abrasive, too independent, maybe, to make the inner circle. She uttered her often unseasoned, unrestrained ideas in a loud voice, and the In group was, like the town itself, on the whole conservative and low-key. Never catch *them* handing out anti-war literature to commuters on the station platform in the early morning.

And Anne—well, it was a mystery why Anne, who could move in any milieu she elected, who was positively courted by the Ins, had chosen Marcy, Chris, and Jimmie to be her closest friends. Perhaps because of her wild-haired eccentric brother who laughed at chic cliques and socially acceptable types. "I'd rather cross swords with a real counter-revolutionary," he'd said, "than sink into the tapioca of the Massic River elite."

So what about me? Jimmie asked herself. By nature, and she wasn't proud of it, a loner, she was just lucky that Anne and Marcy and Chris had found something in her to care for. Without them, she'd have gone on as her nature dictated, being agreeable with anyone who was agreeable to her, but never following up an acquaintance or allowing one to be followed up. More into books than people, like her mother? She'd met Anne and Marcy way back in the first grade, and Chris had stormed into their lives a few years later, and Jimmie was happy to be with them, even if Chris's music was enough to puncture an eardrum.

Suddenly, it stopped, and they came out of the separate dreams into which they'd fallen because of the impossibility of being heard over the new quadrophonic system.

As if to get up, Chris moved one leg from the lawn chair to the grass, then put it back. "I think the neighbors have been sufficiently regaled. Actually, they're pretty patient about it. I talked to the ones over there one day and they said at least I was good enough to turn it off by ten—which I usually was and of course always have been since they said that. Awfully canny of them, wasn't it? I do have some marvelous Segovia tapes, Bach, and nice quiet classy stuff if anyone wants—"

"Later, maybe," said Anne. "Let's just sit and talk."

"Did I tell you I'm in this Encounter Group?" Chris asked. "No? Well, it's something else. My shrink put me in it. I mean, I'm still going to him but only once a week now, the other day I'm in the group and he's the leader, or Great Spirit, as some of the kids call him."

"What's it like?" Marcy asked, sounding appalled. "Is it like those horrible Sensitivity things, where you all go around feeling each other and making insulting remarks?"

"There's no touching in this group I'm in. Considering some of the freaks we have, I guess I should be glad it's limited to dialogue. But some of that gets pretty hairy."

"Why do you do it?" Anne asked. "I don't mean you, especially. Why does anyone?"

"It's getting things that are buried in us out in the open."

"Maybe some things should just stay buried," said Marcy.

"No. Not according to my shrink. He says we have to dredge up all the old gunk and heal it in the open air of free discussion. My shrink says—"

"Why don't you call him your doctor?" Jimmie snapped.

Chris beamed, as if at an advanced student. "Now, that's just the way it works! You start talking, and all of a sudden someone who's been putting on a show of courtesy and amity suddenly shoots out this little spark of hostility, that maybe that person didn't even know was *there*, and off we go!"

"Off you go where?" Jimmie asked, restraining with difficulty her irritation at having been accused of putting on a show of courtesy and amity.

"Now, Jimmie," said Chris, leaning forward, "be honest. I mean—what's the harm in letting me know you *resent* what I said? Because obviously you're seething—"

"I am *not* seething."

Chris sat back, laughing. "Anyway, that's how it goes. People talk about things, about themselves, about their families, or about what scares them or what they dream—about anything, and the conversation gets going, sometimes awfully fast—and the idea is complete self-*honesty*, and if you try to fake—*well!*"

"What does that mean? That *well?*" Anne demanded.

"It means the other people in the group won't let you get away with it. Rigorous self-examination, where you don't have a chance to hide behind self-deception, that's how it goes."

"I would hate it," Marcy said. "Absolutely hate it."

"Some of the kids do. I'm not all that crazy about it myself, except I hope maybe between that and the once-a-week session with my shr—my doctor—I may just get my head together some day. I mean, lots of kids have this thing about hiding their feelings, like hey, I don't *have* any feelings, or hey, my feelings are so grisly and different that *no*body ever had any like them. In group therapy you learn there's no such thing as feelings that are just peculiar to you. You learn everybody's got these same hang-ups or even worse, and it makes you feel, you know, not so alone, so freaky." She sighed. "I'm going to get my head together. I just know I am."

"What's the matter with your head the way it is?" Marcy asked.

"My god, if you could *see* into it. I'm just a mass of pain and resentment. It's got me to a point where I can't even read. I mean, I really can't. Like, I can't make out words on a *page*. How am I ever going to be an engineer if I can't read? I put that system up there together out of guesses and memory practically. The instructions might as well have been in cuneiform."

Anne was looking at her compassionately. "I didn't know that, Chris. You never said anything."

"Not to you guys. I never said anything about it before except to Dr. Fish, and the group, of course."

"But why? I mean, how did this happen?"

"That's what I'm trying to find *out*. I mean, now look—"

Chris sat up, pulling the back of her chair from a reclining position to an upright one. "That Sally—she's supposed to be our chaperone tonight, right? Not that we really need one, but anyhow she's supposed to be it. How much have you seen of her, huh? She didn't even have the cookout out here with us. She's in there in the living room right now necking or making out with some creep from St. Xavier's that she picked up last week at the Redi-Rooster, and she wouldn't even care if we *saw* her. And I'll tell you another thing—we had a kind of inter-family thing here at Easter and there were, what with all the cross-hatchings or cross-matchings or whatever you'd call them, about sixteen kids, and only *four* of them were still with their original parents. My mother's sisters have both been married three times. Duclair is only mother's second, but already she's looking over his shoulder for a third, I just know she is, although with the way she looks and behaves I can't see how she *finds* them. And as far as my *own* father goes—he has visiting privileges with me and he's never been to see me, not *once,* since they split up six years ago. Sends me a check every Christmas and a present on my birthday. In six years he's sent two watches, three monogrammed pins, and last year he sent a Peanuts lamp. He's even forgotten how *old* I am. And I'm supposed to be in one piece? Or even in a few easily assembled pieces?"

There was a pause, and then Chris said, "Doesn't anyone want to respond to that?"

"Respond how?" Jimmie asked.

"You could tell me I'm full of self-pity. Usually they say 'drowning in it,' but that's because verbally this group hasn't hit its stride yet."

"It sounds to me as if you had reason to be full of self-pity."

Chris gave a hoot of laughter. "You don't get the point, any of you."

"I think I get what the point's supposed to be," said Marcy. "I only happen not to like it. I think—" She stopped.

"Okay, okay," said Chris. "*Tell* us what you think."

"I think people should be kind to each other."

"You know, Marcy, it might do you good to attend a group thing. I mean, how do you know that all this gentleness and meekness you show to the world isn't a put-on? Maybe underneath you're a—a Valkyrie, or something."

"What did the Valkyries do? Took the dead heroes to hell, didn't they?"

"To Valhalla. That wasn't the same as hell."

"It all sounds like hell to me," Marcy said unexpectedly, and the others laughed.

"We'll do it a different way," Chris decided. "Now, I'll ask a question, and then I'll point at one of you, and that one has to answer without thinking at all, if she can help it. Just shoot the answer out of her subconscious, okay?"

Nobody said no, so Chris said, "What's the most important asset a person can have?" and stabbed a finger in Anne's direction.

"Beauty," Anne said promptly, adding, "anyway, a good appearance."

"And how do you justify that sort of superficial-sounding ideal? I mean, maybe it isn't at all. Maybe it has profound significance for you, but would you care to say anything more?"

"I care to say I think this is dumb," Anne muttered.

"*That's* legitimate," Chris said encouragingly. "Go on."

"Oh, really," Anne said, laughing. "I think you're having us on, Chris, that's what I think."

"Maybe. Maybe not. Maybe I don't know myself. But do you want to embroider upon your answer? Expatiate, as Dr. Fish likes to say?"

"You mean defend it, like in a debate? All right. You take a squirrel—"

"A squirrel? Okay, so we'll take a squirrel."

"Now, people aren't repelled by squirrels, in fact they feed them in the park and like it when the squirrel comes to them and takes a nut out of their hand. And why? Because he's cute. And he's cute mostly because of that flashy flirty tail. A squirrel's tail is a very handsome article of apparel, so we overlook the fact that without it he'd really be a rat. He probably *is* a rat. Rodent. But he looks sweet and rats do not, so we feed the squirrel peanuts and poison the rat. See? It's all in appearances. *You* tell *me* you don't respond to a good-looking person, male or female, before you do to an ugly or awkward one. I wouldn't believe you if you did tell me that."

"But that's just an initial reaction," said Marcy.

"Of course. And handsome is as handsome does and all that, and I know handsome guys and some pretty stellar looking girls that I wouldn't give the time to, but that's *after* you get to know them. Chris didn't ask what's the most important quality or character in a person, she asked what's the most important *asset.*"

"I'll tell you what I think," said Marcy. "I think—If this were an exam, I guess I'd have to say a good mind. I suppose I mean a sound mind. If you don't have that, it seems to me, it would be like groping around in the dark with a flashlight that's about to go off."

"But since this isn't an exam?" Chris prodded.

Marcy smiled self-consciously. "Then I'd say the best asset a *girl* could have would be to measure 5 feet 2 and let the flashlight go out."

Even Chris couldn't think of anything to say to that.

CHAPTER THIRTEEN

For some time Jimmie had been sitting quietly, arms across her chest, not participating. She didn't feel well and didn't want the others to know. Her stomach ached, her head ached. Her whole body ached. I must be getting the flu or something, she thought, wishing she were home in bed and not here having a fascinating conversation with her best friends on this lawn where it was getting cold and was already dark.

What a dopey thing to happen. It could have been so much fun, and by the hour it was getting harder to endure.

"I'm cold," she said when only the lights from the kitchen windows made the figures of the four girls discernible.

They went inside, avoiding the living room, still occupied by Sally and her boy from St. Xavier's, and up to Chris's room, where the conversation and the music went on. And on. They had spread their sleeping bags out on the thick yellow carpeting—Chris democratically electing to bunk down on the floor with them—but no one gave a sign of being sleepy.

Somewhere past midnight, Sally poked a disheveled head in the door and said a yawning good night. "You kids okay, aren't you?"

"Sure. Anne cut off a finger accidentally while slicing the melon," Chris said. "But we patched her up."

"Good. Well, sleep tight, all of you."

"Thanks for chaperoning us," Anne said sweetly.

"Oh, I *loved* it. Feel free to ask me any time. 'Night again." She was gone.

"Was she being sarcastic?" Anne asked Chris.

"I know not. She's always like that. Preoccupied, you know. She's a sex maniac and her brain's the merest *pebble*. No matter what you say to her, she answers as if you'd just complimented her on her shade of nail polish. Nice, but so what."

"How peculiar."

"Everybody's peculiar. Want to go down and get some milk and cookies, now that the Redi-Rooster Romeo is gone?"

Well, this night has to be over some time, Jimmie told herself, sitting with them in the brightly lit kitchen, sipping milk she didn't want, thinking longingly of her own room, her own bed. She wondered, all at once, what Goya was dreaming right now. She could see his little form curled under the blankets which he shared with thirteen stuffed animals. This afternoon, just before she'd left to meet Anne, he had come across the lawn, a daffodil in his mouth like a yellow-bowled pipe, puffing in a sedate imitation of their father, and had said, "Now, you have a good time, Janine, and behave like a little lady," in a sedate imitation of Grandmother Prior. Jimmie had hugged him close, smashing his daffodil pipe, and Goya, reverting to his own character, had said, "That's all right, Jimmie. There's lots more flowers."

What I think, she said to herself now, is that the most important asset a person can have is a nice disposition.

"Jimmie," said Anne, "do you realize you haven't uttered for ages?"

"Yes. No. I mean, I know." She forced a yawn, wishing she could ask for an aspirin. "Tired, I guess. I'm sorry."

"Cripes," said Chris, looking at the electric kitchen clock. "It's three thirty. Maybe we should turn in, huh?"

A little later, huddled in her father's old sleeping bag, knowing she couldn't sleep, Jimmie fell asleep, only to waken shortly with the paralyzing conviction that she'd wet herself. She lay still, her face burning, wondering how such a thing could have happened, how she could possibly conceal the mortification of it from the others. Then cautiously she touched a finger to her inner thigh, which was tickling, and realized that now, at this inconvenient time, she was at last menstruating. Relief that it was that and not the other was at first so great that she shuddered, but then the problem of what to do now overwhelmed her.

To begin with, she'd have to get out of this awful, sticky bag. Tucking her nightie between her legs, she eased out of the sleeping bag and made her way by the night-light to Chris's bathroom, closing the door softly behind her before she turned on the light. Only—what to use? Where did Chris keep whatever it was she used? What to do with this bloody nightie? How could she get back in that wet, bloody sleeping bag? What—*what* could she do about *anything?*

"Oh, this is unbearable," she whispered aloud, and sat on the toilet, quietly crying. It was all too much, and she just could not cope.

"What's up?" Chris asked, coming in and closing the door behind her. "You sick?"

"No, I—I just started to—I'm *menstruating*. And I don't know what to do about anything!"

"Boy, you sure look forlorn, sitting there. You don't have anything with you?"

"No, I don't! This is the first *time*," she sobbed, pulling a couple of tissues from a box beside her to blow her nose.

"First time? Wow."

"I know, I know. I'm *backward*. I wish I were so backward I'd never got it at all. Not ever in my whole life."

"Now, don't come all unglued. Aunty Chris will fix. Here—take that washcloth and wash yourself off. I'll get you a pair of pj's. Here's a belt and a pad. You can get them on yourself, can't you?"

Jimmie giggled. "Yes, Aunty. I can do that for myself."

"Good. Back in a sec."

She returned by the time Jimmie had got herself into the equipment she'd read about and passionately longed one day to have use for. So, now the day was here. At that, she thought, it could have occurred under worse circumstances. Suppose she'd been in class? On the bus? How did girls face this problem? How anticipate it? How could you *know* when it would happen, or where? How, short of wearing a napkin every day from age eleven on, could you be prepared? It was really terrible, traumatic—

"Here's some pajamas," said Chris, interrupting her thoughts. "Just stick your nightie in the sink with cold water. You can rinse it in the morning. Always remember —cold water for blood."

"I know. I've read about it." Jimmie shivered a little.

"You'd better have a couple of these—" Chris handed her two white tablets. "For cramps. And get into my bed for the rest of the night. What's left of it."

"I'm sorry you were disturbed, Chris."

"Oh gosh, I didn't mean that. I was just stating a fact. I was glad to help. I just meant you'd feel better in bed."

"Did the others wake up?"

"Out like lights. I guess a person notices something going on in her own house, that's why I woke up."

"Boy, am I glad you did. I'd probably just have sat there and cried till morning."

"You okay now?"

"I'm fine."

" 'Night, then. Or, good morning. Oh—and welcome to the club."

Jimmie·lay in Chris's bed, exhausted, unable to sleep. Now that it had happened, she could admit to herself how horribly afraid she'd been that she'd turn out to be some sort of scientific grotesquerie, that one woman in a billion who never menstruated at all. That she was never going to be like other girls, other women.

She began to smile a little. She was tired. She had cramps. Her head ached. But she was, *incontrovertibly,* a woman.

A light dawn breeze was lifting the curtains into the room and in a branch just outside the window a blue jay offered his fluid, flowing, bell-like song to the waking world, or, probably, just to his mate. A lovely song, the blue jay's, and most people didn't even know he had it.

Listening to his variations on a theme, she looked in the pale light at the three sleepers on the floor. It was good to have friends.

She fell asleep with the morning.

CHAPTER FOURTEEN

The school term ended in mid-June, and while there were those obliged to attend graduation exercises (teachers, the principal, Mr. Beggs, the senior class—not all of whom attended, obliged or not) for the freshmen it simply meant that one day there was school and the next day there was not, and would not be until after Labor Day.

Full summer now.

The feeder was removed from Jimmie's little balcony, but, if she rose early enough, she was able to see catbirds splashing in the birdbath. Able, too, to hear the potpourri of song as feathered virtuosi celebrated the building of nests, the laying of eggs. "The aubade, the morning song," Grandmother Prior had said to Jimmie, "is, to my mind, more beautiful even than their vespers."

Grandmother Prior's old-fashioned house had a morning room with long French windows facing east, and in the summer she sat there drinking coffee, pouring from an old silver coffee pot into a cup that was part of her Lowestoft Queen's ware inheritance. (Most of it was carefully packed away to be, one day, Mrs. Gavin's inheritance, when, Jimmie felt sure, it would remain carefully packed away to be, one day, her own inheritance. She had not decided yet what to do about the Lowestoft Queen's ware when it got to her.) Grandmother, on summer mornings, would be in her morning room, with her coffee, by five-thirty, for the sole purpose of listening to the birds singing in her garden and in the woods behind her garden. She had done this since she'd come, as they said in books, "to the house as a bride some forty years before."

Jimmie and Goya had always liked their Grandmother Prior's house. To visit. It was on the edge of a small town in upstate Connecticut, and had glories to offer. A walled garden that, basking from morning till dusk in sunlight, bore blooms that Dr. Gavin, for all his love and labor and patience, could never achieve because his garden was in the shadow of the house for too much of the day. There were birds to be seen around Grandmother's that at home were only found in Peterson's Guide. Indigo buntings, swallows, flocks of bluebirds that hovered over the meadow grasses as if they'd studied hovering from hummingbirds. And there were hummingbirds, little airy gems sipping at blossoms all day long. There were insects that they almost never saw at home. Butterflies like Japanese fans, and grasshoppers, and fireflies turning greenly off and on in the dark. They'd seen owls there, moving like great brown moths to their nests in the early morning. They'd frequently seen deer, who fled at their approach, white tails flashing, but would return if Jimmie and Goya sat very quiet.

And all of this, to Jimmie and her brother, was the very recipe of joy.

Grandmother Prior's house was wonderful, too. It had a "verandah." This went across the front of the house and all along one side and had rockers on it, and two gliders covered with green sailcloth. Inside there was a big square entry hall with an open stairway going up the center. It had faded flowery carpeting and gleaming brass stair rods. Upstairs, the rooms were large and serene and old-timey, with braided rugs and handmade quilts, pictures in oval frames of long-ago relatives (but no picture, anywhere, of Grandfather Prior), four-poster beds, and white cotton curtains that were over fifty years old and had to be starched and ironed.

Downstairs, the living room, the morning room, the library, the dining room, were like pictures in volumes entitled *Old New England Houses, Interiors and Exteriors*.

Carved mantels, oriental rugs, antimacassars. The polished surfaces of Grandmother's tables shone like dark pools of water and the oil paintings on her walls were dark, too, and heavily framed.

Grandmother Prior had a real maid, Portia, who lived in the house, and a gardener-chauffeur-handyman, Mr. Hunter, who lived over the garage that had once been a barn. Both Portia and Mr. Hunter were as mad for order as Grandmother was.

Something in Jimmie responded to this house, to its poise and air of imperturbability.

Whenever Mrs. Gavin said they were going to visit their Grandmother Prior, Jimmie and Goya were elated. They could hardly wait to get there. And could never, ever, get home soon enough.

"I do not understand," Grandmother Prior had said once, "how you people can turn anyplace you live into a tenement just about overnight."

"The house isn't a tenement. It's simply not a museum," her daughter had replied.

"The fact that I keep my home reasonably ordered does not make it a museum."

"It's unreasonably ordered, Mother. All it lacks to make it Mount Vernon is ropes across the chairs."

Mrs. Prior had sent her eyes traveling slowly around the living room where this conversation had taken place.

"Why doesn't Mark do orthodontia?" she said suddenly. "Dentists *can* make money. Heaven knows, mine must be a millionaire."

"Are you having braces made?"

"Don't be silly. I was just pointing out that orthodontia is a lucrative aspect of dentistry."

"It's also a very specialized branch of dentistry. Mark would have to go back to school, full time. We can't afford that."

"Why didn't he become one in the first place? If he was going to be a dentist—"

"He wasn't going to be one, he is one. And since I'm married to him, I'll do whatever complaining needs to be done."

"You never complain," Grandmother Prior had said, as

if her daughter had let her down badly in this area. "I've never heard you complain about your married life."

Jimmie, who'd been about twelve years old then, had suddenly advanced on her grandmother and, standing directly before her, said shakily, "Don't you dare criticize my father, you—you old bag!"

Mrs. Prior's eyes had flown open, and she turned to her daughter and said, "Are you going to permit her to speak to me like that?"

"Jimmie," Mrs. Gavin had said. "Do you feel like apologizing to your grandmother?"

"Does she feel like apologizing to my father?"

Mrs. Gavin turned to her mother with an air of interest. "How about it, Mother?"

Grandmother Prior had risen, visibly shaking, and looked from one to the other of these females of her line. "I'm going home," she said, and suddenly tears were rolling down her cheeks. "I am going, and I shall not come back."

Mrs. Gavin, still leaning back in her chair, had seemed to be waiting. She said nothing, just watched her mother and her daughter and waited.

"Oh, for Pete's sake!" Jimmie burst out, feeling that her grandmother, this grandmother, was one of the unfairest human beings she had ever known, and that her mother ran a very close second. "All right, I apologize!"

That done, she'd run from the room, feeling close to tears herself. What was wrong with her mother that she'd never stick up for Daddy? Never, for that matter, stick up for her children, or herself either? Why did she just loll back and let such things be said?

I don't care if she does go and never comes back, Jimmie had said to herself hotly. I wouldn't care if I never laid eyes on the old saggy bag of a hag again. In her room, lying on her bed—why did people always have to lie down to be unhappy?—she let herself cry for a little while, then rolled to her back, sniffling. Dumb, dumb people, all of them, everybody, the whole stupid ass of a world was stupid, stupid, stupid—

"Come in," she snapped to someone knocking.

"Hi, honey," said her father, coming in and sitting in a chair near the bed. "Problems?"

"What else, with that old creep in the house."

He shook his head. "Jimmie, Jimmie—"

"Don't Jimmie me. You don't know the things she says."

"Of course I know the things she says. I can't speak for everyone in this house but I, for one, am not a fool."

Jimmie's lips quirked. She burrowed under her pillow, found a handkerchief, and blew her nose loudly. Taking a deep breath, she lay back again and stared at her muraled wall. "Are you practicing to be some kind of saint or something?"

"Say, that's an interesting angle. I wonder if that could be the answer."

"Okay, you tell me what the answer is, will you? Grandmother is horrible to you."

"Not *to* me."

"Then about you. Even sneakier. And Mother—" She sighed gustily. "I don't think she cares what anybody says about anybody. I can't figure out what she cares about, except her stupid indexed books and who's the senator of the month to hate most." Her father didn't answer and in a few moments Jimmie began to feel uneasy. "Why are you here, anyway?" she asked, unable to keep from sounding irritated.

"Oh—I heard sounds of a skirmish and went in and found your grandmother all alone in the living room, crying."

"What was Mother doing?"

"She wasn't there."

Jimmie sat up. "Now, that's just the sort of thing I mean. Goddarn it. Her mother bawling downstairs, her daughter bawling upstairs, and where's she got to? What's she doing?"

"I don't know. I only came in here to see if you were all right. Did you hurt the old lady's feelings?"

Jimmie giggled. "Not as much as that would—you calling her an old lady in that *kindly* fashion. That'd space her out for good," she said with relish.

"Why do you want to space a lonely old lady out for good? How would it make you feel any better?"

Jimmie, turning her head a little, looked with careful

scrutiny into her father's face. "You really truly mean that, don't you?"

"Of course I do."

"But she's so ghastly about you. About all of us. She says we live in a tenement, and that you're not even a good dentist because you don't make a lot of money— and what she thinks of a person becoming a dentist in the first place—"

"Spare me," said Dr. Gavin, holding up his hand. "I know the script by heart."

"Then why don't you hate her?"

"Hating upsets my digestion. It makes the world an even colder and more frightening place than it already is, and that's bad enough. I tried hating when I was much younger and found it wasn't helping me in any department. I just can't accommodate the emotion."

"You don't even hate your enemies?"

"Jimmie—I don't have any enemies."

"Grandmother Prior is your—"

"Don't be silly. She's a vain lonely woman who expected to conquer worlds and wound up a deserted wife whose only daughter is married to a dentist. She's embittered, and I feel sorry for her."

Grandmother Prior's husband (my grandfather, Jimmie had thought queerly, not remembering him at all, nor her other grandfather either since he'd died years ago) had, a long time before, when Jimmie had been a baby, asked his wife for a divorce, which she, naturally, refused to give him. Failing to get the divorce, Grandfather Prior had opted for plain freedom, going off one day with a suitcase full of clothes, his sterling silver flute, and half the bank account. He'd been to a lawyer and given all else he possessed, which was apparently a lot, to his wife, who was thereby left "comfortably off," and miserable. But Mrs. Prior had kept her chin up, remaining in the same house in the same town, which, Dr. Gavin said, required a certain kind of courage.

Nobody knew where Grandfather Prior was now, and it was all mysterious and sort of sad. Jimmie found herself softening toward her grandmother.

"Well, I guess she finds it pretty hard to be happy," she said to her father.

"I'd say she finds it impossible. But then, I'm not sure she tries to be happy. The women in her family—" he began, then broke off and they both pretended not to know what he'd been about to say.

"Do you know what Abraham Lincoln said about happiness?"

"What?"

"He said, 'A man is as happy as he makes up his mind to be.' That's good, isn't it? He meant a woman, too, of course."

Jimmie liked various watchwords and slogans, which she wrote in a school notebook with a marbled cover. It was nearly half full and in those days she'd planned to reorganize it, when she had time, into a sort of Daily Book. She would have 365 pages, and at the top of each an uplifting or thought-provoking sentiment, leaving room underneath for her own observations. A diary of attitudes, not activities.

She looked at her father and said, "Do you suppose she's really going to leave and not come back? Grandmother, I mean?"

"I imagine she doesn't want that. But she may be forced into it by pride. She is helplessly at the mercy of that stiff-neckedness of hers."

"I guess I better head her off."

Dr. Gavin had smiled. He had a beautiful, a radiantly loving smile. In Jimmie's estimation, an unparalleled smile. "You are a daughter in a million," he told her.

Her heart so filled with love and tenderness for her father that it easily spilled over to include others, Jimmie went to challenge her grandmother to a game of Scrabble, which, after a moment's hesitation, Mrs. Prior agreed to.

Goya came in while they were playing, and with unconscious ease leaned against his grandmother's chair, one small hand on her shoulder. "That's good, Grandmother," he said when, from their behavior, he guessed that she'd made a successful play.

Jimmie, glancing covertly at this beautifully groomed, youngish-looking (despite what her father had said) grandmother of hers, from whose face all trace of tears had been erased with skillful make-up, thought—Well, this is probably as close to happiness as she can get. She felt proud of herself for having brought the present state of things into being. With, of course, a little assist from her father.

But that day was two years in the past. Grandmother Prior had continued to visit, alternating her times with Gram, and nothing much had changed except that Jimmie and Goya had got older. (Grown-ups didn't seem to get older—not noticeably, the way children did.) Jimmie had stopped adding to her Daily Book, a thing, like the doll house, she'd outgrown. Their own house got shabbier. If he had ever been going to be a rich dentist, Dr. Gavin had passed the point when he should have started. His practice now consisted mainly of poor people, and it appeared that once you got a reputation for having the poor in your waiting room, the rich preferred to wait somewhere else.

"Maybe I made a mistake," he'd said to his wife recently, "in not leaving the Building when so many other dentists and doctors moved to that new place outside of town. I should've got a new office, maybe, instead of just a new chair and the speed drill."

The "Building," was the Beggs Building, and it was in the business district of the town, with bad parking facilities, and a dwindling occupancy. It was not modern and stylish at all, as was the new medical complex just outside town, where people could park easily in a parking lot that had a fountain splashing in the middle, with flowers around it, and after getting their teeth cleaned could shop in beautiful branches of New York department stores.

There were no beautiful shops near the Beggs Building. Just moribund Main Street shoe stores, delicatessens, and empty stores with fly-specked For Rent signs in dusty windows.

"Why don't you move now?" Mrs. Gavin had asked, managing to sound as if the decision was entirely his to make, as if she had no stake, no interest, in what the decision might be.

He'd sighed and said that at this point his entire practice, practically, used city transportation and most of them couldn't get to him in the new place.

"Wouldn't you get new patients?"

Could anyone, Jimmie had asked herself, overhearing this conversation, read into her mother's question anything except polite uninterest? No, she answered herself, no one could.

Her father had said, "That's just the point. Maybe I would and maybe I wouldn't. I guess maybe I'm afraid to find out. And then, I sort of like my old patients. I have a responsibility to them, wouldn't you say?"

Help him! Jimmie had screamed silently at her mother. He is asking you for help, so give it to him! But such a long silence had ensued in the kitchen, where they'd been talking, that she got up from the stairs and went to see what was happening.

Her mother was at the dinette table, reading *Lenin and The West* as if it were a novel. Looking through the window, Jimmie could see her father gently turning the earth in the circular bed around the birdbath. He'd recently cut down the dry dead tulip stalks and planned to put begonias and ageratum and alyssum there.

Not wanting to talk to either of them, Jimmie had got her bike and Goya and had pedaled over to the Massic River, where Goya could throw sticks in the sad and slovenly stream.

"You know what?" she'd said to him.

"What?"

"I think people should be required to take an examination at least as tough as the SATs before they're allowed to get married. And nobody scoring under, say, 500 should *be* allowed. And then everyone, no matter what their score was, should have to wait five years and then take another examination, even harder, before they're permitted to have children, that's what I think."

"My stick's stuck," said Goya.

"In my opinion," she went on, "the profoundest and most perplexing riddle mankind has ever posed itself is whether the chicken or the egg came first. Oh, you can laugh," she said to her brother, who wasn't listening, "but think it over for a moment. Is Mother the way she is—lazy and not interested in anything except books and politics, and how do we know all that flap isn't just a smoke screen to keep us away from her and keep her

away from us and everybody else—she doesn't even have
any friends, do you realize that—because Daddy is the
way *he* is—just sort of happy-go-lucky friendly, except
what good that does him when he can't bring any friends
home, I don't know—and wanting just to work in his
garden and carve nice things and look at the *Million Dol-
lar Movie* once in a while?"

She stopped, breathing hard.

Goya, with a long stick, worked to get unstuck the
small stick he'd launched on the river. "Where do you
suppose my sponge is?" he asked.

Now, a few weeks later, the ageratum and begonias
and alyssum were flourishing in the bed around the birdbath, school was over for the year, and at the end of the
month they'd be going up to Grandmother Prior's for
their summer visit. In spite of past experience, Jimmie
found herself, once again, looking forward to it. She did
not like to leave her father to fend for himself down
here during the week, but he'd be coming up weekends
and would take her and Goya for long marvelous walks
in the wood, where he knew the name of every tree and
plant and shrub, and was gradually transferring that
knowledge to his children.

CHAPTER FIFTEEN

Marcy Beggs had gone to Europe with her mother, for the entire summer. Mr. Beggs had invited her closest friends to ride out to Kennedy Airport with him to see his wife and daughter off. Since Anne had already gone to Castine, Maine, where she spent the summer with her parents, that left Chris and Jimmie to enjoy the long ride in Mr. Beggs's limousine, which was air-conditioned and had a chauffeur and covered the miles creamily. From tape decks came soft music of the fifties, occasionally bringing a smile of recollection to Mrs. Beggs's face. She was still a very pretty woman, not nearly as tall as her daughter. She wore a marvelous travel pants suit, navy blue with a tangerine silk scarf at her neck and some orange bracelets above her right elbow. Marcy, looking uncomfortable in an equally smart pants suit (pink, increasing her resemblance to a flamingo) sat between her father and mother on the back seat. Chris and Jimmie sat on comfortable jump seats, facing them. All this perfumed, musical luxury glided toward the airport and Jimmie found herself wondering what Peter Ferris would have said about it.

Peter had finished college, as he'd promised his father he would, and then shouldered his backpack and started off across the country, not sure where he was heading or what, if anything, he had in mind to do. He had wanted to paint, on the back of his jacket, "I won't love it *or* leave it," but Mr. Ferris had said that for someone who believed in nonviolence, that motto was practically designed to stir it up. Peter had agreed.

The Ferrises were not rich, like the Beggs family, and Jimmie, looking at Mr. Beggs, remembering all his speeches about democratic values and the American Way of Life ("Which is my way, and your way, and let us not, friends and young people, be misled by the lunatic few who would seek to tear down our honorable institutions and bring shame upon our glorious flag—"), wondered, as her father had, what Mr. Beggs would have done with or to a son like Peter. Probably he'd have spent a few years trying to straighten the lad out by sending him to a military academy, or trying to buy him out with a lot of expensive junk. If these methods proved unsuccessful, if Peter refused to shape up, he'd have been told to ship out. Actually, she could not imagine Mr. Beggs having a son like Peter. If Marcy had been a boy, she'd have been a long thin simulacrum of her father (but, just possibly, with her shoulders straight? Because, of course, Mr. Beggs would have preferred to have a boy, and that sort of preferral might just have made the difference between a stoop-shouldered child and a straight-shouldered one) or she would long since have split for good. Mr. Beggs was of The System, for The System, and by The System. In fact, Mr. Beggs and his ilk *were* The System. So he could never have lived with a son in the state of armed affection that endured between Peter and Mr. Ferris.

I really don't like either one of you at all, she told Mr. and Mrs. Beggs, who were too sure of themselves and of their value to receive such a silent message. And you don't have to think it's because you have such a lot of money that I don't like you, because that's not why I don't like you. I think it's probably all right for people to have a lot of money, except it's too bad it works out that so few have a lot and so many have absolutely none at all. No, she went on in this silent confrontation, I don't like you because you have a lovely daughter and you've bent her shoulders through not giving her any sense of *her* value.

Mr. and Mrs. Beggs were talking to each other across Marcy and missed the communication from the jump seat.

At the Pan-Am building, skycaps took Mrs. Beggs and Marcy's luggage from the trunk of the big car, and the chauffeur drove off with instructions to return in an hour. Mr. Beggs then steered his little party through the vast waiting areas filled with common folk waiting, to a large comfortable private room at the back, where they were served coffee by a hostess who greeted Mr. Beggs by name and assured him that the airline would do everything in its power (which you could assume was considerable) to see that his wife and daughter had a perfect flight and if there was anything they could do at the London end, just let her know—

Back there in the waiting rooms had been hordes of young people milling about, shouting, laughing, vibrating with the sense of adventure ahead. There was an electric air of anticipation out there. In here, except for herself and Chris and Marcy, there wasn't anyone under—well, Jimmie couldn't guess at people's ages, but there certainly wasn't anyone who looked like fun for Marcy. Would Marcy rather be out there, Jimmie wondered, in chinos and sandals with practically no luggage, or in here cosseted with the rich middle-aged?

No way to find out that or anything, since Mr. and Mrs. Beggs sat with them, asking polite questions about what Jimmie and Chris planned for their summer, not listening to the answers, but not, either, leaving the three of them alone for a nice farewell talk. Marcy, silent and unresponsive, left it to Chris and Jimmie to entertain, if that was the word, her parents.

"I'm going to be working in a day-care clinic," Chris was explaining to a smilingly inattentive Mrs. Beggs. "It's volunteer work, of course, because somebody my age can't get a job that pays. In fact, young people generally are having a terrible time finding work. The economy is such a mess," she said unwisely.

That caught the attention of Mr. Beggs. "I'd venture to say that it was more the young people—a certain type of young person of whom unfortunately we have more and more with us—who are a mess. Look at that spectacle out there—" He gestured beyond the walls of their retreat.

"What spectacle?" Chris asked.

"That mob scene of American youths leaving for the Continent, almost in a state of undress, probably with their pockets full of drugs, to clutter up European cities and give our country a bad name. For every young American who looks like Marcy—or you girls," he added unconvincingly, "there are a hundred of those slobs to represent us. It's no wonder Americans aren't popular abroad."

Jimmie and Chris exchanged glances, and Marcy stared at her feet.

After a long pause, Mrs. Beggs said to Jimmie, "And have you any summer plans, dear?" She turned away and lifted a gently summoning hand to the waiter. "Hot coffee, please," she told him. "And do empty that ashtray." She looked at her husband. "I'll stop in Piccadilly and have some of your cigars sent over, shall I?"

"Do that. And be sure to let me know the moment you—"

Jimmie wondered why they had asked Chris and her to come to this pitiful bon-voyage celebration. Marcy didn't want them. She had gone into some unreachable place and didn't know they were there. Mr. and Mrs. Beggs were having a stunningly cosmopolitan conversation full of expressions like, "When you get to the Crillon, Yves will be there to meet you," and, "Don't let Marcy talk you into Saint-Tropez, we don't want her with that sort—"

Poor Marcy. As if she'd talk her parents into or out of anything, and what was the sort they didn't want her with?

The conversation—". . . Cannes . . . the Havermeyers' yacht . . . if you see anything in that—what was the name of that gallery in Rome we liked? . . ." continued between Mr. and Mrs. Beggs. Once he started to say something, and with a warning glance she whispered, *"Pas devant les enfants—"* and Jimmie nearly choked.

Still, it was impressive, in a way, and surely not intended to impress. So what are Chris and I doing here? Jimmie asked herself again, and had a feeling she'd known before, that the present situation was past alteration, that it had gone on too long ever to change, that she would, for the rest of her life, be here in this dully exclusive place with these dull middle-aged exclusive people—

"That's your plane," Mr. Beggs said, rising, dropping his cigar in the ashtray, tucking the amber holder in his breast pocket. "Got everything? Good, let's go, then."

There was one thing to be said for seeing off first-class passengers, they got to go on board before the second-class, and so those seeing them off got to leave first. For a moment, Jimmie was afraid that they'd have to wait to see the plane actually take off, but Mr. Beggs turned away as soon as his wife and daughter disappeared into the plane.

"Long ride back, girls. The car'll be waiting."

It was. Mr. Beggs got in front with the chauffeur, leaving Chris and Jimmie to ride in style behind a glass partition with the music still softly playing and the smell of leather and *luxe* and some lingering fragrance from Mrs. Beggs surrounding them.

"Do you suppose this thing is bugged?" Chris asked.

"You mean can he—" Jimmie gestured with her chin toward the front seat "—hear us? He seems to be on the *telephone*." Suddenly Jimmie twisted around to look through the back window at a taxi going past the other way. "Hey, Chris—there was Dick!"

"Dick Mosher?"

"Yes—driving right past us in his cab. Isn't that amazing?"

"Why? He's a taxi driver, and they come out to the airports a lot, I should think."

"I know, but that we should see him. That's amazing."

"Did he see us?"

"No, and it's just as well. He might think we'd been seduced by the establishment."

"Too bad Anne wasn't here. Oh, no—she's all over her passion for him, isn't she?"

"She couldn't bear not to be reciprocated."

"Give her a few years and everybody in sight'll be reciprocating."

Jimmie sighed. "Yup. She's awfully pretty."

"Oh, now—you're pretty, too," Chris said, in a tone so crassly consoling that Jimmie laughed. "No, you are," Chris went on. "Different type, of course."

"How?"

"Well—my analysis of Anne is that she'll always be absolutely sure of herself, or as sure as people can get, and will always be pretending to some man that she only just survived until he came along. Whereas you—"

"Well?"

"Oh—I think you'll always be pretending to be sure of yourself but hoping for some guy to take over."

"Huh. Thank *you*, and all that."

"One thing you have to learn, and that's not to get your feelings hurt when somebody answers something you've asked."

"My feelings aren't hurt. I'm just telling myself you could be wrong."

"Sure, I could be. Probably am."

"What about you—have you analyzed yourself?"

"I'm waiting for Dr. Fish to give me my end-term report. Now Marcy—boy, I wish I could've got her to go to the group. She'd be a smasher, if she'd straighten up and get some confidence in herself. But she has to have *help*."

Jimmie scowled toward the front of the car. "He might hear," she whispered.

Chris hesitated only slightly. "Well, if he does have the back room wiretapped, he could maybe hear a few hairy home truths. But it's probably safe as cheese back here. The Beggses aren't going to ride around letting the help in on their spats."

"I don't see how putting Marcy in that bear pit you call the group could help her. It seems to me people must crawl out of it feeling like segmented worms."

"That's only in the beginning. After a while, after you've got some confidence in yourself, you don't let the insults or the criticism bother you—you just tell yourself whatever they're saying is their hang-up, not yours."

"But then what's the point of the whole thing?" Jimmie asked. "If you're there to listen to honest criticism but then don't pay any attention to it what good can it do?

And how do you get the self-confidence at all? I mean, how do you *get* to that part, past all the insults and criticisms? I just can't think that anybody's character ever got improved by—"

"It isn't supposed to improve character. The sessions are basically supposed to help you live with the character you have, and not get all uptight about it. Acceptance, that's the keynote. Of yourself, and of 'your essential helplessness as one individual in an increasingly confused society.' That's Dr. Fish. You learn to live with it. Your character, and all the rest."

"I do live with it. I don't have to go get maimed by a bunch of people my age who've slipped the leash and been told to go for the jugular. I know I'm just one helpless individual in an increasingly—complex, did you say?—society. I don't have to get beaten up to accept it. Or my character. Such as it is, I've settled down to live with it. I don't need help from a bunch of teen-age exterminators."

"You see how it works? Now *you* are being shirty about something that means something to *me*—namely, my Encounter Group. You're putting it down without really knowing what it's like. But do I get mad? I don't. Because I say to myself that—"

"Oh, hey—I'm sorry, Chris, really I am."

"You don't have to be sorry. It was perfectly natural. I mean, you said something that you honestly believed, and it also happened to come out sort of crabby and condescending, but honesty often does come out that way, which is why people tend to avoid it when they can."

"Maybe it's just as well," Jimmie said. "I think that's always been my only point in putting the group down, Chris. I think that being honest usually does hurt people. I don't know why, and I suppose thinking like that leads to all sorts of horrors, like lying to someone for their own good . . . Oh, I don't know what I mean. Except I'm sorry if I hurt you."

"But you didn't," Chris insisted. "Actually, seriously, and I'm not too sure, if you want to know, just how serious I *am* about this group—I just sort of got into it on account of Dr. Fish and then got interested enough to hang around because something might help me stick the bits and pieces together and maybe it just *could* be group therapy instead of the vis-à-vis kind—" She stopped. "What was I saying?"

"You said 'seriously,' and then got sidetracked."

"Oh, yeah. I remember. Well, there's one thing I have got out of going to these sessions, that's for sure. I've learned that nobody can hurt your feelings unless you let them. If anybody says or does something that might hurt you, you just simply keep saying over and over to yourself, 'that's his problem, that's her bag, it's nothing to do with me.' "

"Suppose it does have something to do with you?"

"Mostly you'll find it doesn't. I mean, people only say hurting things to other people because of something inside themselves they're afraid of, so they lash out."

"But when you're lashed out at, sometimes it cuts, no matter whose bag it is."

"Only if you let it," Chris said firmly. "For my part, I do not permit just *any*one to bruise my spirit or maul my soul."

"Golly."

After a while, Jimmie asked, "Are you getting so you can read? You said that was why you started going to the doctor, because you couldn't read."

"I went because my head is like a platter that fell off the top shelf. Well—sort of. I mean, I can look at a page of print without getting a pain in my stomach. That's progress, I suppose. If I don't learn to read again, I'll never get out of high school, much less to college."

"I suppose you have to go to college," Jimmie mused.

"I do," Chris said promptly. "I have my reasons. Did you get invited to Castine?" she asked.

Jimmie, surprised by the abrupt change in subject, nodded. "I don't think I can go. Did you?"

"Yes, and I'm going if I have to hitchhike. I've *got* to get away from the step-relatives and the drunken slop I listen to all the time. I hate drunks."

They glided across the George Washington Bridge, up the Palisades Parkway, off the Parkway, along Route 502, onto the Massic River Road, and so into town. Mr. Beggs, after a bit of difficulty in getting one of them to pick up the car phone, asked if it would be all right to drop them downtown, he had an appointment which would make it inconvenient for him to—

"Sure, sure, Mr. Beggs," Chris said into the mouthpiece. "That's fine. Just hang a right at the corner and let us off."

Jimmie took the telephone from Chris. "We want to thank you for giving us such a lovely outing, Mr. Beggs. It was really barfy."

Mr. Beggs signaled his satisfaction through the glass, gestured to the chauffeur, who pulled up to the curb immediately. He did not get out to assist Jimmie and Chris, who stood on the sidewalk watching the long car flow away from them.

"What a square," said Chris laughing. "But what a thing to say, Jimmie. Suppose he'd known what it meant?"

Jimmie, a little ashamed now, said only, "Poor Marcy."

Their buses went in opposite directions, and Chris's came first.

"So long, Jimmie. It's been real."

"Yeah, it always is. See you."

When her own bus came, Jimmie found a seat and sat back, sighing. *Your essential helplessness as one person in a confused society.* Was that how it had gone? And wasn't it all worse, more confusing, if you were young? People their parents' age had problems all right, but by then wouldn't you be sort of used to having them?

A few months ago it had got all around school, in the way things that ought to be private get around, that Faith Powers had tried to commit suicide. She'd gone down one frigid sleety night to the banks of the Massic River, planning to lie down and freeze to death. Why, you ask, would a young girl, veritably a child, wish to do such a naughty? Oh, come now, that's *easy*. This child didn't have any friends to play with. With her lies and her airs and her phony high spirits she'd managed to carve a place for herself in the *Now* world of youth where she was absolutely positively all by herself. Alone. Do you hear that word? Alone. Nobody can stand being alone. People die of being alone. Faith had tried to die of it. Faith—the rumor went—and how did these things get around? Had Faith herself told?—Faith had spent several days trying to *will* her heart to stop beating. But the heart is an un-muzzled muscle, strictly its own boss. It can't be told when to beat and when to stop beating. A person could want, with every fiber as they say, to have an end put to this ceaseless pumping, this day in day out, night in night out, thudding of an organ that just by its own persistence keeps all the rest going. But no effort of the will impresses the heart. In a book her mother had given her, *Out of Africa*, Jimmie had read that the Masai, a tribe in East Africa, could dictate terms to the heart. The Masai were never imprisoned because none of them lasted in prison more than two or three months. No one knew how they brought it off, but a Masai, in three months or less of physical incarceration, gave up the ghost, instructed his heart to stop, and it stopped. Still, what could be achieved by the Masai in the bush was no go in Massic River, New Jersey, so failing that, Faith had left a note on the pin-cushion and gone down to the river bank to put an end to it all. But, and this was the joke that went around the lockers, she'd worn ski pants and boots and a fur parka, people said, to be warm while she froze to death. Faith, it seemed, was laughable. The police found her and took her home and she didn't even get the sniffles. She did, however, get put in the hospital and had been there ever since. What kind of hospital? A mental one, of course. Some people do go mad. Some get drunk. Others sniff, pop, or drop. Chris had gone to visit Faith in the mental hospital. Anne and Jimmie had gone there, once, together. Trying to atone for being all too humanly unkind to some-one who no longer cared about their kindness or their lack of it.

What did people do with all the pain that came of living? What, when you came down to it, could they do, having got started, but just keep on, if they didn't choose drink or drugs or self-destruction?

"Your mother," her father had said one day, "suffers from dysphoria."

"Gosh. What's that?"

"A pervasive sense of discontent and ill-being."

"Your father," Mrs. Gavin had said on a different day, "is like a cork. He just has to keep bobbing to the surface, no matter how troubled the waters are beneath. He can't help it, I suppose."

What did people do?

Goya, when she got home, was sitting on the bottom porch step, chin on his fists.

"Hi, love. What're you doing?"

"Thinking."

"What about?"

"School. I have to start going to school, now I'm five. I don't want to. I want to stay home." Goya had successfully fought off nursery school, but the Gavins had decided that this fall he'd go to kindergarten, willing or no.

Jimmie sat beside him. "Don't feel like that about it, darling. School is fun. You'll be with lots of other children—"

"Will Kenny be there?"

Did he or did he not think Kenny's presence would be a comfort? How should she answer? Not being able to read his mind in this instance, she was obliged to fall back on the truth.

"He'll be there. Kenny has to get an education, too, you know."

"Will he learn to read?"

"Certainly, and so will you. You're going to love being able to read. Only you must let me go on reading to you, too. Because that's my pleasure."

"I know," said Goya. "I bet I don't learn to read as fast as Kenny does. He already can say the alphabet to K."

Kenny had gone briefly to nursery school during the spring, but had been expelled as an incorrigible.

"That's nothing," Jimmie said. "I can teach you to say it right through. And to count, too, if you want."

Goya pondered, sighed deeply. "All right, Jimmie. But I still won't like it."

"Why start worrying now? It's ages away. Ages."

That seemed to strike the right chord. Goya brightened and asked if she wanted to read to him now. "You can read me the *Tale of Two Bad Mice*," he offered. "I love the part where Hunca Munca and Tom Thumb break up the pudding, the lobsters, the pears, and the oranges. 'There was no end to the rage and disappointment of Tom Thumb and Hunca Munca,' " he quoted happily. "—'*bang, bang, smash, smash!*' "

Jimmie laughed, but wondered how you were supposed to bring nonviolence into a world where it started in Beatrix Potter?

Her father came out on the porch.

"Jimmie, your mother and I would like to speak to you."

Nailed by fear to the step on which she sat, Jimmie stared at her father.

"Will you come in, please?"

Goya scowled. "Jimmie's going to read to me. She's going to read where Hunca Munca and—"

"Later, Goya. Not now. Come on, Jimmie. Please."

She got up, running her hands, the palms suddenly moist, down the sides of her skirt, and followed him into the house with an icy, empty feeling in her chest.

CHAPTER SIXTEEN

"I tell you, I can't stand it!"

Jimmie stood in the middle of the living room, fists doubled, tears streaking down her face. "I can't stand it, and I won't! I don't care what you two want, I won't put up with it, do you hear? You can't do this to me and Goya!"

"But, Jimmie—"

"No, no, no, *no!* What's the matter with you, are you crazy? How can you want a divorce after sixteen or whatever years of being married? If you've been married that long, what difference does it make now anyway? Why now? Why not six months ago, or six years ago? What do you think you're *doing?*"

Her mother sat, motionless, expressionless, on the sofa. Her father was in a chair, his face in his hands.

"Look at me! Answer me!"

"Let him answer," said Mrs. Gavin. "He's the one who wants this divorce. Get the whys and wherefores from him."

"Well?" Jimmie yelled at her father. "Do you know what you're doing to us?"

He lifted a pale and unfamiliar face. He looked sick. He looked like someone melting, disintegrating. "I know one thing," he said. "I know I have to get out of this. I can't stand any more."

"Can't stand, can't stand!" She advanced on her father.

"This is because of that—that creature you've got sharpening drills down at the office, isn't it? *She's* the one who's breaking up a perfectly happy marriage. Isn't she, *Daddy?*" She stopped to draw a breath.

"A perfectly happy marriage," Dr. Gavin said. "That's what you said? A perfectly happy marriage. *Come off it,* Jimmie. You're smarter than that. I'll tell you something —*nobody* breaks up a perfectly happy marriage. It can't be done. Furthermore, if you think that's what your mother and I have been sharing, I don't know where you got this reputation for brains."

Jimmie was stunned. Her father on the attack was— was incredible. It was having a supporting beam yanked out, so that her world tilted toward destruction. The strangeness of it almost silenced her, but then the monstrousness of what was happening drove her into protest again. And even as she shrieked and defied them, she knew there was no point in fighting because this battle had been lost before she even got into it.

"You didn't answer me, *Daddy.* Are you divorcing us to marry that—that *harlot?*"

"Jimmie!" he said sharply. "Don't demean yourself this way. I forbid you."

"Oh. You forbid me, do you?"

"Yes, I do. In the worst, in the very worst human situations, some kind of restraint is required, do you understand? You are to exercise some, and that's an order. Do you understand that?" Abruptly he leaned his head back, closing his eyes.

Jimmie, boiling with ugly words she wanted to spill on him, on both of them, held her tongue, saying to herself, *Some kind of restraint, some kind of restraint.* Queerly, it was like clinging to a log in a tossing ocean.

Her father opened his eyes and looked at her. "This— marriage—your mother and I have, is just not bearable. We tried—" He lifted his hands. "I don't care whether you believe me or not, I'm simply telling you that we tried, and it won't work."

"A pretty sudden decision, isn't it?"

"No. It isn't. It's been a decision in the making maybe since we got married."

"Then why did you *get* married? Why didn't you find out it wouldn't work before you had children?"

"Would you want not to have been born?"

"That's precisely what I'd want."

"You say it, but you don't mean it. You're bitter and angry just now, but you're too healthy and full of life to—"

"Now you knock it off!" Jimmie screamed. "Don't give me your half-assed philosophy—"

"People of limited vocabularies always resort to vulgarity in time of stress," said Mrs. Gavin. "It's their only recourse."

Jimmie wheeled on her. "You're something else. You really truly are. How do you dare talk to me that way while you pull up my whole life, and Goya's, by the roots?"

"I have to use words when I talk to you," Mrs. Gavin replied, her voice shaking. Her breast was rising and falling rapidly, and now and then she opened her mouth and seemed to snatch at the air.

"And just what, *may* I ask, and *if* you two don't find it too much trouble to respond, being otherwise engaged—say, that's funny, isn't it? People get engaged to be married, so do they get engaged to be divorced?—Well, maybe it isn't funny. But could I ask if anybody's given any thought to what happens to *Goya* and me? Do you draw lots, or divide us in half? I only ask because I need to know, you know. Don't mean at *all* to pry into your personal affairs, which apparently don't concern *us* at all—"

Dr. Gavin exhaled a huge breath, choking on it slightly. "You'll live with your mother, both of you. Naturally."

"Why naturally? What's natural about it? What's natural about any of this?"

"Would you rather live with your father?" Mrs. Gavin asked. She had her spine pressed against the back of the sofa, and seemed to be trying to push into it even farther.

"I don't want to live with either one of you! You're cowards and traitors and unfit—unfit—" She sank to the floor. Her throat hurt, and her chest. Hiccoughing sobs tore out of her like screams, mixed with hysterical trickling laughter.

When, from exhaustion, she'd quieted, Mrs. Gavin said in her ordinary, calm tone, "Your father was trying to be thoughtful, to answer your question about why now and not at some earlier date. He waited, he says, until you'd finished the school year and until you'd—got your period. He didn't want to say anything until he was sure you were all right."

"All *right!*" Jimmie shrieked. "Oh, he has sure been thoughtful. I mean, I could write him a *thank*-you note if I had the right kind of stationery. He's fixed it so I couldn't be all righter, all right."

"He did what he thought was best for you, under the circumstances."

"And what are you doing, being so *understanding?* I think you're absolutely weird. Why don't you come right out and *say* you don't like him?"

Mrs. Gavin shrugged. "I don't. I think he's a self-serving louse."

"And you've been a darling ideal wife, I suppose?"

"I guess," Mrs. Gavin interrupted, seeming almost to appeal to her husband, "we have to put up with this because of what we're doing to her?"

He sent his sick man's gaze around the room. "I guess we do."

"Not me, you don't have to put up with anymore," said Jimmie. "Because I'm going upstairs to get out of the sight of both of you."

In her room she was taken by a fit of trembling, and then had to go down the hall to the bathroom to be sick. While she was washing her face with cold water, then trying to rinse the acid sour taste from her mouth, her mother knocked at the door.

"Jimmie. Jimmie, please. Let me help you."

"You can't help me. You just leave me alone, that's all. Leave me alone!"

In the nights that followed, when her father had left them to take a little apartment—a squalid apartment, Jimmie found it—downtown, she often heard her mother wandering around the house, going restlessly from room to room.

One stormy night, Jimmie crept down the stairs and walked through the dark to the kitchen, where only the light over the dinette table was on. The rest of the kitchen was in shadows, and her mother sat, drinking tea, under the lamp which she'd dimmed to its lowest point. She looked up, trying a smile.

"Want a cup?"

"No." Jimmie hovered, shifting from one foot to the other, in the doorway. "I'll have some milk." She got a glass and sat across from her mother, and for a long time they didn't speak.

Mrs. Gavin stared into her cup as if the future might actually be read there. Jimmie looked out the window, watching occasional flashes of lightning that quivered in the sky like strobe lights. Rain beat down in the darkness, and where the kitchen light fell on the andromeda bush that pressed up to the windowpane Jimmie could see its drooping leaves and dingy blossoms gleaming wetly.

In the past week she had found that anguish and rage and disbelief seemed all to be emotions that had limits. When she stopped to remind herself of what was happening (and the unimaginable thing was that now and again, for a little while, she forgot, or let it slip and hide in some corner of her mind) she would feel a spasm again of fury, of betrayal and incredulity, but each spasm was shorter, less stabbing. It was almost as if her body, or mind, or spirit, or whatever, couldn't support so much emotion but gave way, bringing a kind of resentful peace in its place. Which, in itself, seemed a betrayal.

"You can't sleep," she said to her mother at length.

"No."

"What are we going to do, do you know?" She congratulated herself on how she was exercising restraint.

"Sell the house. And then, I guess, we'll move in with my mother. If you can bear it."

Jimmie shrugged. She wondered why it had apparently never occurred to her mother, in her whole life, that she might get a job, the way other women did. She'd gone from college back to her mother's house, and now was going back to it from marriage. It was not a question she was prepared to put.

"What it comes to is that your father can afford to give us an amount of money that by government standards is on the poverty level."

"Are you taking alimony, Mother?"

"No, Jimmie. I am not taking alimony. I am taking support, and very little of that, for you two children. I suppose I could hold out for more, but then what would he live on?"

"He and Emily Copeland, you mean?"

"I don't know anything about that. You seem to. He's never said anything to me about her."

"I don't *know* either. Only why would he—why would a man—what does he want a divorce for at all, if it isn't another woman?"

A threatening roll of thunder suddenly was the real thing, detonating in the air with one sullen explosion after another. Mrs. Gavin's cup jerked in her hand, spilling tea.

"I know nothing about your father's plans," she said, mopping her saucer. "I know just one thing, and face just one thing, and that is that our marriage is finished and I have to decide what to do with myself. And with you both. You and Goya."

Jimmie shook her head, which was aching. "I just do not understand, and I'll never understand."

"All you need understand is that two people who lived together find they can't anymore."

"Then why did you decide to live together to begin with?"

"Jimmie—sometimes you seem so old to me, so mature, and then you'll say something to remind me of your age, which after all is only fourteen. Do you really think that people can figure out ahead of time, for a lifetime, their entire needs and wishes? That's what the marriage contract is. That's what it asks. That two people be absolutely sure, with no doubts or reservations of any kind, that they are going to feel a certain way about each other all the rest of their lives. You *can't* promise feelings."

"Did you ever love each other?"

What a strange way to be talking, in the dimly lit kitchen, in the dark early morning in the storm, with her mother to whom she had never spoken about anything real before. Or had she? Hadn't she, years ago, gone to her mother when she wanted to get a bit of knowledge, or help, with which to face the world? When had her mother retreated into that cool, unknowable place, taking with her comfort and counsel for her children? When she'd found that she couldn't keep the promises of marriage? That would have made it quite a long time ago that the dissolution of this marriage contract had begun.

I never really thought it was a happy marriage, Jimmie told herself. I suppose I just thought they'd devised a way to be comfortable with their unhappiness. Or, if not comfortable, resigned.

"Did you," she insisted, "ever love each other?"

"I think so. I'm not sure, now. As I remember it, the way I remember it, we did. But in a way, I suppose, I married him to get away from my mother."

"Well, that's a darling thing to say."

"I thought you were so smitten with honesty? I'm paying you the respect of trying to be honest, as long as we are having this talk. I'm trying to—clear things up for you. As well as I'm able. And plenty of women have married to get away from home. But yes, I loved your father. That kind of crisp cheerfulness he has. I loved that. What Romain Gary calls a 'pioneering disbelief in people's ugliness.' I've always believed in people's ugliness. That your father couldn't, wouldn't, see it—that charmed me, made me love him. Then."

"Do you ever have an original thought? Must you always duck behind quotations?"

"Other people have said what I think so much better than I can."

Her mother took bad temper, abusive talk, mildly. Not, Jimmie thought, as if she were being forgiving. She acts as if it couldn't matter less, what is said to her, even by her daughter.

She felt gritty with resentment.

"I suppose I should apologize," she snapped. "I'm being pretty snotty."

"I guess you feel you have a right to be."

They listened to the rain falling. The kind of rain, Jimmie realized, that her father always said was good for his garden. Her eyes were stinging. What would happen to his garden now? This house, that she and Goya had always lived in—who would live in it now?

"When do you—I mean, how do you get a divorce? I mean, who gets it, him or you?"

"I will. I'll fly to Mexico in a couple of weeks. It's quicker that way. Just get it over with, that's the idea."

Jimmie was sickened. Flying to Mexico for a quickie divorce. Her mother. A horrible jet-setty sort of thing to do. Only, what would be better? For her mother to go to Reno and hang around gambling casinos, being picked up by cowboys, like in that sad movie about the horses with poor dead Marilyn Monroe?

"How do we sell the house?"

"Put it on the market. I did that, yesterday. I warn you, Jimmie, it'll be awful. People walking through our rooms, looking at them, sizing them up, poking in the closets, rejecting us—" Mrs. Gavin shivered. "Awful."

"Suppose nobody buys it?"

"Somebody will. Somebody always buys, if the price is right."

As so often happened with her mother, the words seemed to mean something other than what they said. Jimmie found herself not interested enough to puzzle out the meaning here, and maybe, after all, there wasn't any. Maybe that was just the way her mother sounded, and there wasn't any other meaning at all.

She thought of going to bed, but her mother just sat, listening to the rain, so Jimmie stayed with her.

Presently Mrs. Gavin stirred and said, "Did you ever read that verse of Housman's '—*To think that two and two are four/And neither five nor three/The heart of man has long been sore/And long 'tis like to be.*' It seems to me people spend their lives trying to make it five or three, but it keeps on coming out to four."

"Then why not accept it? Settle for four."

"I don't seem to be able to. I keep wanting it to be five or three—"

Her voice was dreamy, her eyes blank, and Jimmie felt a pang of pity, and of apprehension. Surely—surely *re-*

alistic people didn't go on wanting two and two to be five or three?

"Mother," she said briskly, "I think we ought to try to clean the place up. I mean, if people are going to be prying and poking—"

CHAPTER SEVENTEEN

House agents began arriving at all hours with prospective buyers. Jimmie hated them all, with their chilly appraising eyes, their prying and poking. One woman even opened the medicine cabinet.

"It's just like any other medicine cabinet," Jimmie snarled. She'd been following the woman and the realtor, as she followed everyone who came to the house, in a spirit of masochism. "Maybe it's cleaner than some," she added.

She and her mother had cleaned the house, and by their standards had cleaned it well. It had taken Jimmie a whole morning just to get the stove presentable, and she began to see what Grandmother Prior had meant.

They had scrubbed and polished and thrown things out and washed windows and floors and cleaned the medicine cabinet. All in a week.

"I want to get it sold and get out," Mrs. Gavin had said. "I feel as if I were living in a—" She'd broken off, but Jimmie could have finished that sentence, because she, too, felt as if she were living in a tomb. Only, what was it going to be like, living at Grandmother Prior's? Living in that big, still, gleaming house, instead of just visiting and then getting home to the comfort and sloppy ease of home? Grandmother Prior's museum would now be home. So, Mother got married to get away from there and sixteen years later is going back, the worse for one

154

marriage, the better for two children. Jimmie had tried a sardonic laugh. It emerged a snuffle.

How do people get through life? she asked herself now, watching the two women, the skeptical buyer and the eager seller, go into her father's study, empty now of his things, of his spirit. Just how do people contrive to do that—get through life?

Oh, I want to die, she moaned, and went into her room and fell on the bed.

She didn't cry, but lay with an arm across her eyes, and said to herself again and again, "How do they do it? How do people get through life?"

She wondered what Gram was doing, what she was feeling now. Gram had written a little note to Mrs. Gavin, sort of like a condolence letter, but it hadn't really said anything. Gram, probably, had to be on Daddy's side. In a divorce, everybody chooses up sides. Except I can't, thought Jimmie. I'm stuck in the middle. She couldn't not love her father, not want to see him, have him near, turn to him, laugh with him, hear him laugh. But since that night when she and her mother had sat in the shadowy kitchen and listened to the storm and talked to each other, she realized that she was not going to be able to do as she'd secretly planned—just wait until she was sixteen, when the law gave her the right to choose, and then announce that she preferred to live with her father. If he hadn't married that creature, and he said he had no plans for marrying anybody. If you could believe him.

But now she wouldn't be able to do that. She had a feeling that her mother needed her, which was a funny way to feel about a woman so emotionless that you'd think she wouldn't need a thing but her books, her bed, and maybe some intravenous feeding from time to time. Just the same, Jimmie did feel it. And in two years, Goya would need her. Maybe more even than now.

Again, the effort to believe that any of this was actually happening seemed to rise up like a glass wall that she repeatedly crashed against.

She rolled to her stomach, moving her head against the pillow, wondering if it was possible for a person to smother herself. Who could you believe or trust, anywhere?

She pushed her face into the pillow, trying to keep it there, trying, as Faith Powers had once tried, to force her heart to stop beating. But it beat on, and in a very short while she had to lift her head and gulp in air. One night she'd gone into the bathroom and got a bottle of fifty aspirins and a glass of water, intending—had she really intended?—to swallow them one by one and get out of all this mess and pain and fury. She'd shaken out a few, then carefully put them back in the bottle.

She'd thought of Goya, asleep with his thirteen stuffed bed companions, confident of his sister's living companionship the next day. She'd remembered that her father had visiting privileges with them, that she'd be seeing him, able to hear his voice, feel his arms around her. If anything went awfully wrong, she could call him and he'd be there. Instead of divorcing them, he might have *died*. "No matter what happens," Anne had said once, when Peter had been in an automobile accident and had had to spend weeks in the hospital in traction and plaster casts, "you can always figure that something worse might have." Anne had been right. She might now be mourning her father's real *forever* loss. But he was alive, still there for her when she needed him, and he would always love her, divorce or no divorce.

If he didn't marry that creature.

She found herself thinking of the day she and Marcy and Anne had walked through the churchyard and stopped by the grave of Willow Farnham, only sixteen, and dead a hundred years now, plus a few. Willow must have had her problems, too, her seemingly unendurable burdens. She must have been perplexed and baffled and undermined with despair at times. And she must at times have been happy. And now it was all one, all nothing, for Willow. She'd got through her life. If Willow could do it, Jimmie said to herself, I can do it.

And she didn't—probably—have to die when she was sixteen. She'd told her father that she'd rather not have been born, and she'd said to herself that she wanted to die. But she didn't mean either. She just wanted it not to be now. If it could only be a *year* from now—

"May we come in, little girl?"

The real estate agent, wanting to look into this last room with her prospective client.

The day they'd told her of the divorce, Jimmie had put a sign on her door. *"Do Not Enter. No Time. No Way. No How."* But she'd had, of course, to take it down.

"Little girl," Jimmie snorted, and called, "Just a sec." She got up and straightened the bedspread, glanced around the room, and went to open her door to the two women.

"My goodness," said the client, her eyes falling on the doll house. "What a magnificent thing. Is that hand-*made?*"

"My father made it for me."

"Oh—oh, yes." The woman's eyelids fluttered in confusion, making it clear that she understood the circumstances under which the house was being sold. "Well, it's a beauty," she said, and turned hastily to survey the rest of the room. Her eyes, encountering the mural wall, widened.

That'll space her out, Jimmie thought with satisfaction. Wish we'd left Chris's sexy boy on.

"Isn't that simply marvelous?" the woman exclaimed. She turned from Jimmie's cold gaze to the real estate agent beside her. "Don't you think that is absolutely enchanting? What an idea, to let children decorate a whole wall! If we *do* take the place," she said, turning back to Jimmie, "I have a daughter who will simply dote on that."

Jimmie decided to paint the mural out.

The next day, Chris came over, and with pans and rollers they spread a latex cover over the rear views of rabbits, over the sayings, the watchwords, over the tale of Hansel and Gretel painted there with such joy such a long time ago.

Chris talked about general matters—Sally's silliness, a movie she'd been to, a dress she'd bought—until Jimmie said irritably, "Will you please stop acting as if there was nothing going on in my life? *Every*thing is going on in my life, and I don't have a shrink to spill my problems to."

Chris gave her a quick look, and nodded. "Sure. Just

didn't want to climb into your sandpile if you didn't want me there. You feel like talking about it?"

"I don't know."

Jimmie dipped the roller and smoothed it slowly over a message left by Marcy just before her trip. "Farewell friends, I'm off to prance in London, Eng., and Paris, France." The roller went over the words and they might never have been written.

"I hope Marcy's prancing."

"So do I. Say, why did you pick such a yucky color?"

"In case this woman buys it I hope it makes her daughter puke."

"That's the spirit."

Jimmie continued to send the roller slowly up and down the wall. "You could give me the benefit of your experience. With divorce, I mean."

"Well, your case is different. I mean, my mother and her sisters are natural husband-hunters. But I simply can't imagine your mother saying, 'Darling I'm *between* cads. You can't *think* what a relief.' That's what one of my aunts said."

"No, my mother wouldn't say that."

Strange that she hadn't thought, not for a moment, of the possibility of her mother's remarrying. Sometime in the future, probably, she'd have to accept the fact that her father would remarry. He was a man who wanted a home. Furthermore he didn't do things for himself with any skill, the sort of things that must be done if a home is to run at all. Cook, mend, market, clean. Badly as her mother had done these jobs, her father couldn't do them at all. It didn't seem a good reason to get married, but it seemed *a* reason. But, now that she did think of her mother, it seemed to Jimmie that her mother would never marry again.

"To tell you the truth," Chris was saying, "I think most men would be out of their depth with your mother. She's too intelligent."

Too frigid, thought Jimmie.

"Chris, do you ever miss your father?"

"No!" Chris put the roller carefully in the pan, and sat on the floor. She sighed heavily. "Sure I do. Girls can't help missing their fathers, if they aren't absolute monsters, that is."

"I thought you said yours was."

"Did I? I was probably angry or something. No, in a way I don't blame him for cutting out. Would you want to be married to my mother if you were a man?"

"But what about you? He could have seen you, couldn't he?"

"I think, Jimmie, he just wanted out so badly, he needed so much to get away from that woman and her drinking and her men, that all he could do was run. And I suppose," she added simply, "he just associates me with all the rest of the mess and can't face any of it. I sometimes think he even wondered if I *was* his daughter. Sometimes I wonder myself," she said in a soft, vague tone. She stared dreamily at the half-covered wall.

"Oh, Chris. Oh, I'm so sorry."

Chris rubbed the back of her neck and seemed to emerge from a trance. "Don't get upset, Jimmie. I've had years to get used to it. Besides, I'll tell you something I've never told anyone else, not even Dr. Fish. I plan to see him, my father, some day. I'm going to see to it that I go to some college out West, any old college, so it's far enough west. And then I'll simply arrive on his doorstep one day and say, 'Father, here I am,' and he'll throw his arms around me and say, 'Christina, welcome home!' "

"Oh, stop it," Jimmie said. "You're going to make me cry. I spend enough time crying these days."

"What about?"

"What *about*? What's the matter with you? My whole life has fallen apart and you say what about? I'll have to be living up there at Grandmother Prior's, and I'll never have any friends again—"

"Oh, come on, Jimmie. Let's paint. You'll meet loads of people. I bet it'll be fun, in a way."

"You sound like me telling Goya what a gas kindergarten is going to be."

"Besides, we're always here. You can visit. And you can ask us up there. I kind of like your grandmother. I mean, I like both your grandmothers, but Mrs. Prior is a real gutsy girl. You don't give her enough credit."

"You don't have to live in her museum. And visiting—that just won't be the same as you and Anne and Marcy and me being here together, being friends every *day*."

"Stop dribbling into your soup, Jimmie. One thing I've learned from the group, and that's that self-pity is the destroyer. You have to fight it all the time."

Jimmie wished she had never been critical of Chris's Encounter Group. Chris had plenty of really mind-bending problems, and she faced them, tried to cope, tried to plan. Chris never whined. And her grisly Encounter Group apparently did help her.

"You know," Chris was saying, "it's too bad I'm going to Castine so soon. I mean, I could put it off, if—"

"I wouldn't think of it. Besides, we have to start packing and all. I'll be busy."

"Your mother's going to Mexico?"

"She is," Jimmie said glumly. "Next week."

"Be gone a couple of days, then. Is somebody going to stay with you and Goya, or are you—"

"My grandmother, Daddy's mother, is coming," Jimmie interrupted.

"Is this one of those friendly divorces you read about but I don't believe in?"

"No. They're fighting over money and furniture and god knows what. But on the surface they pretend to get along. For Goya's and my sake, I take it."

"How's Goya taking it?"

"Couldn't care less. I don't think he even knows what's going on."

"Well. Five years old. What do you expect. Do you realize we've got this wall finished?"

Jimmie looked at the ugly bile-green expanse and her eyes filled again with the too-easy tears of the past days. "Don't pay any attention to me. I do this all the time. Dribble into my soup. You know, I hear people laughing lately sometimes, and I think to myself, how can they? How can there be anything to laugh about?"

"Jimmie, take my word for it, you'll get over this. What you want is for this part of your life, this time of it, to be over, that's all. But it will be over, and you will have friends, and something to laugh about. I mean, honestly. I *know*."

"I'll never have friends again like Anne and Marcy and you."

"Well," Chris said modestly, "quite possibly that's true. There, you see—you're laughing already."

"Oh, let's clean up here, Chris, and get on to the next slide, shall we?"

"Suits me."

They washed out the rollers and pans in the bathroom, took them down to the cellar, and then carried iced tea out to the back yard, where enraged shouting from Goya and Kenny could be heard at the other side of the bayberry hedge.

"Well, there is one blessing, just one," said Jimmie.

"The last of Kenny?"

"The last of Kenny."

They smiled and sipped their tea. After a while Goya plunged through the opening in the hedge, closely followed by Kenny, who drew up short when he saw Jimmie.

"Get lost," she said. "Back. Back through the hedge. We've got smallpox here."

"Jimmie, you know what he did?" Goya wailed.

"No. I don't wish to know, either. Go wash your face."

"But—"

"Go and wash your face."

Goya went, stamping and yelling, banging the screen door behind him. Jimmie lifted her shoulders and looked at Chris. "Maybe he doesn't know *what's* going on, but I guess he knows something is. Goya's not like this, ordinarily. That little crumb Kenny is always bawling and yelling, but Goya, no—"

"Jimmie, I have an idea," Chris said brightly, pushing aside the matter of Goya and Kenny. "A very good idea."

"What?"

"I think you should start calling yourself Janine when you get up to your grandmother's. A new name for a new life. It seems very appropriate. Besides, you don't really want to go through life with an epicene name, do you?"

"I certainly don't. It sounds awful."

Chris gave a satisfied nod. "Means common to both sexes. In other words, you can't tell which sex it is, from the name. I was afraid you might already know, and it does me so much good to know something you don't, once in a while. What do you think of my idea?"

"It makes your name epicene, too. This new definition you've taught me."

"So it does. Okay. Janine, my friend, you will please to address your friend Chris by her proper name, Christina, in future."

"So noted."

Another long silence and then Jimmie said, "I just thought of the funniest thing. I mean, it's funny I should think of it."

"What's that?"

"At my Grandmother Prior's house, the water pressure is so good. I mean, showers and baths in her house are real. We've always had terrible water pressure in this house."

"There, you see," said Chris. They looked at each other and burst out laughing, and Jimmie was terribly, horribly, sorry that her father took just that moment to come around the side of the house and find her laughing with a friend. As if nothing were wrong. As if she didn't care what was happening—to him, to herself, to all of them.

CHAPTER EIGHTEEN

"Gram?"

"Yes, love?"

"Tell me, please—what am I going to do up there? How am I going to stand it?"

Her grandmother looked at her steadily, but did not reply.

"I mean," Jimmie went on, "I don't want to say anything against them, and you know I—I'm fond of Mother and Grandmother Prior. But they're so—" She stopped, searching for a word. Gram didn't help her out. Jimmie had known she wouldn't. In Jimmie's recollection, Gram had never said anything against her son's wife or mother-in-law. Come to that, Grandmother Prior didn't *say* anything against her daughter's husband or mother-in-law. All so well-bred, they are, Jimmie thought. So good at keeping their feelings under wraps.

"They're cold," she said defiantly. "And the house is. There's nothing cozy. Grandmother thinks cleanliness comes in *front* of godliness, and Mother is like those people who go into retreats and read about the world so they can tell themselves how right they were to renounce it—"

"Did you think of that yourself?" Gram asked curiously.

"No," Jimmie muttered. "I heard Daddy say it to her one night before he left. She said that was better than being some man's vessel and vassal, which was what *he* was looking for in a woman. They had these fierce quiet fights after Daddy asked for the divorce, when they thought we weren't listening. Of course, they had them before he asked for it, too. I don't know what's the matter with them!" she burst out. "Why did they ever marry each other?"

"People make mistakes, Jimmie. Can't you accept that?"

"It's pretty hard on their kids, that kind of mistake."

"Yes, it is. And you'll have to accept that, too. It's awful, and it happens. Broken marriages are like automobile accidents, or fatal illnesses. You think they only happen to other people, other families. And then you find you're wrong. Your mother and father are quite as miserable about this as you are."

"Are they? Are they, just. All I've picked up is flak over who's getting how much money and who gets custody of the Chinese cabinet—"

"There's never been any question about the Chinese cabinet," Gram said, and then looked abashed.

"You see—even *you're* catching it. It just seems to me they're more worried over dividing up their possessions than they are over splitting up their family."

"Jimmie, Jimmie, please. People—oh, how can I explain this—"

"I'd like to see you try."

"People," old Mrs. Gavin continued, ignoring her granddaughter's hostility, "try to fasten on unimportant things to take their minds off big ones, frightening ones. Except that, of course, no matter if *you* like it or not, money in our world is important. Your mother will require some and your father doesn't make a great deal. The ingredients for ill-feeling are built into a situation like that—"

"Has it ever occurred to anyone," Jimmie interrupted, "that Mother could ease this situation by just plain doing something? She's a perfectly healthy woman, as far as I know. So why doesn't she do what other women do in *situations* like this—get a job? Why doesn't she learn to drive a car and go out and get a job and be in the *world*, where the rest of us are? Might even cure her insomnia, *I* think, if she ever did anything but read and try to get back to sleep—"

"If you go on this way, you are going to make yourself sick."

"That might be an idea—in lousy novels didn't the child used to go galloping up to death's door and that brought the parents back together knowing all along they'd truly loved?"

"You think there's a possibility of that here?"

"No."

"Then try to be—oh, Jimmie please, please, try to accept what's happened. Try not to be bitter. Your parents are human beings and they made a human mistake and are doing what human beings do to try to rectify that kind of mistake. They're both young still, maybe they can make lives for themsel—"

"Are you trying to tell me Daddy wants to get married again?"

"I'm not trying to tell you that!" Mrs. Gavin lifted her voice. "I am trying to get you to face with some—some maturity—a thing that you have to face anyway. I am trying to help you," she said, almost whispering now.

"Oh, Gram!" Jimmie threw herself against her grandmother and felt consoling arms go around her, felt her grandmother's lips on her hair.

"There, there, love. There, there. Everything's going to be all right."

"Is it?" Jimmie sobbed. "I'd love to believe you. Only how?"

Mrs. Gavin patted the glossy head that lay against her shoulder. "If you would give these two poor people a chance, Jimmie. If you would try to be grown-up a little earlier than you'd expected to be, and see their side."

"Why are you so grown-up?" Jimmie asked wearily. "I mean, it isn't because you're old—I mean, older. Some people never are grown-up, but you are." She straightened and smiled weakly. "Madame, I see you have in this bowl an excellent batch of maturity. Would you care to divulge the recipe for our listeners?"

"Recipe for being grown-up?" Gram said seriously. "If there is one, I suppose it would consist of large doses of understanding, and compassion, I suspect. And smaller doses of—good humor? Objectivity? Does that sound about right?"

Jimmie smacked her lips. "Tastes *excellent*. Perhaps just a *touch* more seasoning?" She sighed. "Nothing like a metaphor, is there, Gram?"

"Sometimes they help."

"Will you tell me something?"

"If I can."

"Why aren't you—why are you still seeing my mother's side? She made your son miserable. Aren't mothers supposed to hate the women who make their sons miserable?"

"Hate. That's an emotion I couldn't support."

"Daddy said that to me once. More than once. I guess he learned it from you."

"From me, or his father. From life. From himself. You asked about being grown-up. I don't think grown-up people hate."

"What about things that are hateful? People that are? What about Hitler? People who are cruel, who are in a position to hurt other people and do it? What about them?"

"You despise their acts, you fear them, you try to work against their wickedness. But hate in the human heart is an evil in itself."

"You know, Gram, I practically never disagree with you about anything, but I disagree with you and Daddy about hate. I think there's room in the world for hate, because there's room in it for wickedness. Gram—don't look at me like that. I'm not talking about my parents. I know they aren't wicked, and I couldn't hate them. I don't *know* anyone I could hate. Not even Kenny. I just say I think it's possible."

"Darling, won't you please try to eat?"

They had been packing all morning and now were sitting on the living-room sofa with sandwiches and milk, untouched, in front of them on the coffee table. Mrs. Gavin, young Mrs. Gavin, was in Juárez, and Dr. Gavin was no doubt at his office. Goya had tried to help them for a while, and then had left for one of his many parting forays on the house next door.

There were labels on the various pieces of furniture and on the crates and boxes. All books to go to Grandmother Prior's, all records and tools into storage for Dr. Gavin. The study furniture and the Chinese cabinet that Jimmie loved and the stereo equipment, the living-room carpet and a silver coffee service that had belonged to Dr. Gavin's parents went into storage. The rest of the silver, china and glassware, and some of the other furniture, like the things in Jimmie's room, were going to Grandmother Prior's. Anything left over was going to be given away, since Dr. Gavin said he didn't want it, and Mrs. Prior said she wouldn't have it.

"I wonder," Jimmie had said earlier, laying a card that read, "For Storage," on the Chinese cabinet, "why they care so much about dividing up this stuff. I think if I were getting a divorce, I wouldn't want anything, not one thing, left over from a life I hadn't wanted either."

"Well," Gram had said sadly, "you couldn't expect your mother to give up her books, or that set of lithographs she's so fond of. And your father's just keeping his music and tools and some things that come from an even earlier life. Perhaps there's an element of bitterness—"

"Perhaps?" Jimmie had snorted. But at her grandmother's expression, she'd tried to check her own bitterness, only to let it flood forth an hour later.

"Okay," she said now, picking up her sandwich. "You eat, too, Gram."

They ate silently, without relish, and then Jimmie said, "Don't worry about me, Gram. I shouldn't have said all that, and honestly, I'll be fine. Grandmother Prior is okay. I've always liked her, in a way. And Mother—who knows? She got real peppy for a while there, when we cleaned the house so the real estate people wouldn't be ashamed of us. Maybe it'll last."

"Maybe. I have known people to flourish, once the trauma of getting a divorce was over." She fetched up a great sigh and stared at the wall opposite, where pale rectangles betrayed the absence of the three Chagall lithographs that had hung there so long.

"Maybe I shouldn't say this," Jimmie began, and plunged on before her grandmother could stop her, "but it seems sort of cruddy to me for Mother to be taking money from Daddy at all. After all, her mother has plenty, and—"

"Jimmie!"

"Okay, I was just saying—"

"Your mother is not taking alimony. Just support for you children. She insists on that, and I think she's right. Your father would not have it otherwise. He isn't going to have your Grandmother Prior assuming the care of his children."

She's going to be assuming a darn good part of it, Jimmie thought. "Gram, when you say 'your Grandmother Prior' that way—are you *sure* a smidgin of something like hate doesn't creep in?"

"Quite sure. I don't much care for her, but that's because she has never cared for my son. I do not hate her."

"All right, Gram."

Jimmie looked, with some surprise, at her empty plate and glass. "Oh, darn—I *am* going to miss the Chinese cabinet. Grandmother doesn't have *anything* Chinese in her house."

Gram's husband had believed that no house was complete without at least one piece of Chinese furniture. The ebony cabinet, with its lovely inlaid mother-of-pearl garden scene, had been the great extravagance of his life, and it seemed to grow more beautiful with the years. Yes, she was going to miss it. She hoped it wouldn't be in storage too long.

"Is Daddy going to stay in that ratty little apartment?"

"Only until he decides what he is going to do. He needs time to think."

Jimmie opened her mouth, closed it again. She would not, absolutely would not, mention Emily Copeland again. Ever.

"Well, I hope it won't be long. That he has to stay there. It's awful. Gram?"

"Yes, love?"

"I—I mean we—Goya and me—we can come and visit you?" She wondered how. Would Grandmother Prior and her mother agree to send them to Michigan now and then? Gram could hardly visit up there. "When you come to see Daddy, can we see you?"

"I couldn't live, not seeing you and Goya."

"And Daddy—you don't think—I mean, it isn't *pos-*

sible that he wouldn't want to see us, is it? I mean, my friend, Chris—Christina—her father walked out the door after his divorce and never looked back. He went out to California and has never seen her or sent for her once in the whole six years he's been gone."

"I know. You told me. It makes me ill, just to think of. But he must be a very peculiar man. A real wretch. Jimmie, you know your father loves you and Goya. He'll want to see, and be with you, and—Oh, dear." Mrs. Gavin closed her eyes as tears welled from them and trickled down her cheeks. Jimmie, not knowing what to do, finding nothing to say, took one of the knuckly hands in hers. It was cold.

"Oh, Gram," she said mournfully. "My Gram, I'm sorry. Don't cry. Really, don't. Everything's going to be fine, you'll see—"

Gram cleared her throat, wiped her eyes, and said, "We seem to have reversed roles. Of course everything is going to be all right. As all right as things get in this far from all right world."

This was so unlike her grandmother's customary, almost unquenchable, optimism, that Jimmie's spirits sank. No matter what they told each other, each in turn trying to brace the other with assurances that everything was going to be fine, her grandmother's troubled expression and her own sense of loss and anxiety prevented her from believing that anything was ever going to be fine or all right again in her world.

What *right* had they to do this? *What right?*

"Gram? Gram, I'm talking to you!"

"What is it, Jimmie?" Mrs. Gavin asked in a tired voice.

"Can Goya and I come and live with you? We—I—don't want to live with—I don't want to be with any of them. Please, Gram, tell me we can—"

"I can't tell you you can, because you can't." Mrs. Gavin was now definitely crying, quietly, miserably, like an old woman.

Jimmie, sitting hunched beside her on the sofa, felt a wave of resentment against the whole adult world, Gram included. They couldn't handle anything, couldn't help anybody. It frightened her, thinking that way, but it was their fault, all of them.

What are we going to do? she asked herself in silent and mounting despair. What are Goya and I going to do?

She hadn't seen her father for nearly two weeks now. She missed him. Missed his voice, his smile, the unfailing certainty of his presence in her evenings. It seemed to her that she went about all her days sick and full of torment, feeling as if the world had come to an end—as her world certainly had. Nights spent crying, twisting on the bed in actual pain, often seeing the dawn break, were turning her into a person like her mother, who slept very badly and said so in the morning.

Chris claimed she could never remember the sound of people's voices when she was away from them, but Jimmie found that she had an acute recall for the sound of her father's voice. She could hear him, in her mind, saying silly things, dear things, saying, as he had one time, "It's sweet to be loved, Jimmie," and adding, "almost as sweet as loving." She kept remembering that.

She remembered him sitting in his little study, under a powerful light, using an old dentist's drill to draw fine lines down the chess queen's skirt. She remembered one day last summer when he'd taken her and Goya to Jones Beach—a hot, sunny, sandy, hot-doggy, splashing, shouting day it had been, and she'd wanted it never to end, not ever, not ever—

Mostly she remembered him in his garden. Not in the summertime when it was in full bloom and he was weeding, pruning, sweating happily for hours. The picture in her mind was of her father standing in the garden in the early spring or late winter, looking with an expression of whole and perfect joy, of love, at the dark sleeping earth, knowing where every flower would bloom, every shrub flourish, every bulb thrust upward into the light.

What's going to happen to his garden now? she thought. What's going to happen to him without a garden?

"Gram?"

"Yes, Jimmie?"

"I'm going to see Daddy."

"Now?"

"It's Wednesday afternoon. He doesn't have office hours Wednesday afternoon."

"Shouldn't you call first?"

"No. I just want to go there."

"Suppose he's not there?"

Jimmie hesitated. "Then it'll be Fate, telling me I'm not meant to see him again."

"Jimmie, how can you say such a thing?"

"I mean—Fate saying I'm not meant to see him today. Can I go, Gram?"

"All right. You'll be back for dinner?"

"Sure."

She ran to the garage, wheeled her bike out, and was on it and off before her grandmother could have second thoughts.

He was in. Jimmie, knocking on his door, her heart knocking, too, heard the sounds of the Water Music. Her father always said the Water Music would cheer the halls of hell.

He opened the door, and his expression, which was expectant, altered somehow, but was still welcoming, though surprised. She didn't try to work out the meaning of his look but just walked into his arms and sighed, her head against his shoulder.

"I got to thinking about you," she said, after a moment, moving away from him and into the room. "So I thought I'd come to see you."

"I'm very glad."

The music was coming from a little radio. "That's new," she said.

"Yes."

"You must miss your stereo."

"I do. It isn't what I miss most, but I miss it."

Jimmie turned to him, her eyes brimming. "You prefer this ratty room and loneliness to us."

He looked at her in silence and it occurred to her that he looked older than he had even a few weeks ago, *before that day*, when if you judged by the results, he'd been just as miserable, as unloved, as lonely as he was now. Except of course, for his children. They had loved, did love him. Apparently children, when the divorce comes around, don't weigh in very heavily . . . Oh, we *love* the kiddies and all that—too bad they have to suffer—not their fault poor little tykes—but how much worse for them in a home where discord—etc., etc., etc.

"Why are you looking at me like that?" her father asked.

"Sorry. I was thinking."

"I could see that. I wonder if you'll ever forgive us."

"I wonder, too."

"Do you want to sit down?"

She looked around, sat in a canvas butterfly chair that was not very clean.

"This is what they call a furnished apartment?" she asked.

"Seems it is."

"I hope you don't stay here very long."

"I don't think I could. It's—"

"Squalid."

He nodded.

"I was thinking, earlier—I guess it's why I came here, really—what are you going to do without a garden, Daddy?"

He pulled a wooden chair close to her, took one of her hands in his, and said, "Jimmie, listen to me—"

Snatching her hand away, she squeezed her arms against her sides, narrowed her eyes and said, "Oh, no you don't. I mean, *don't you dare!*"

"But Jimmie—"

She was on her feet and out of the door running, hearing his voice that called her, just once. "Jimmie," he called. "Please—"

She pedaled toward home erratically, dangerously, her blood pumping so that she was deaf to traffic sounds, but with her perfect recall for the sound of his voice, hearing over and over and over, *Jimmie, please—*

At home, Goya said he'd invited Kenny for dinner.

"You *what?*"

"His mother says he doesn't like anything with fat or lumps in it, and he can't eat mayonnaise."

"Well, you just go back and tell them that that's what

we're *having* for dinner. Fat, lumps, and mayonnaise."

She went into her room, and slammed the door, leaving her brother shouting in the hall outside.

That had been in July. In September, Dr. Mark Gavin and Miss Emily Copeland were married, in Michigan, at his brother's house.

Gram wrote to Jimmie about it.

". . . try to understand . . . your father needs love . . . Emily does truly . . . I miss you . . . Jimmie, write to me, please. Jimmie, please . . ."

After a few weeks, Jimmie wrote to her grandmother in Michigan. She didn't mention her father or Emily Copeland. Emily Gavin.

CHAPTER NINETEEN

"Dear childhood friends: First off, as Goya says, let me explain why this letter is addressed to Anne. It is, you may already have guessed, in the interests of fair play. I show no favoritism. Next epistle will go to Christina, and following that, a chapter of the log to Marcy, whereupon we will begin again with Anne. As you can see, I definitely plan to keep in touch and you'd all three better see that you do, too. Now then—I write this sitting in Grandmother's garden. There's a bit of October nip in the air but the sun is warm . . ."

The sun was warm. The dogwood trees were filled with catbirds and towhees who chattered and fluttered as they tore clustered red berries from the branches and gulped them down. There were still flowers in the garden. Spider-flowers, and dahlias and pink rambler roses and red. There was even some leftover phlox, tattered and wispy, and spiky salvia shedding petals like drops of blood. There were hundreds—maybe thousands—of chrysanthemums, and there were marigolds, huge marigolds, pale yellow and pumpkin orange, whose musky scent filled the hazy autumn air. Although acorns littered the grass and continued to fall with hollow thuds, only a few yellow beech leaves had begun to detach themselves from the branches and idle earthward. The hills in all directions were checkered and stippled and mottled like a Joseph's coat—scarlet and orange, caramel and plum, green and gold.

Twice since she'd been sitting here in the lawn chair, pad and pen more ignored than used, the Canada geese had gone honking over in wavering wedge-shaped formations. They were beautiful, beautiful, flying low over the town, their wild voices calling.

"How free they sound," Jimmie had said to her Grandmother Prior, who had come out especially to see and hear the wild geese going over.

"And, of course, are shackled by laws more rigid than any of ours, because they can't break theirs. The laws of instinct are immutable in the wild. It's only in laboratories that we can alter them."

"I never thought of that, I guess. I mean, birds are a symbol of freedom, to human beings."

Mrs. Prior, binoculars to her eyes, studied the sky for a long time, then lowered the glasses and said, "I didn't know, when we bought this house, that it was directly in the path of a flyover for so many migrating birds. It has been one of the greatest joys of my life."

Jimmie smiled, and wrote, "Grandmother is here in the garden with me. She's a bird watcher and she's watching birds. You'll be surprised to hear, I guess, that I get along with her just fine—"

Better than I do with my mother, she thought, but didn't write. It appeared that she would always get along better with her grandmothers than with her mother.

One evening recently, after Goya had gone to bed, she and her mother and grandmother had watched an old movie of Sidney Poitier's. *To Sir, With Love.*

Partway through, Mrs. Gavin had moved as if to leave, then glanced at her mother and daughter and sat back again. Doesn't want to spoil our enjoyment by walking out, Jimmie had thought, taking her attention briefly from the story of a classroom of British delinquents who are transformed, by a young black teacher, into mannerly young adults in the space of a year. It was a lovely movie. Just lovely. Jimmie and Grandmother Prior watched the ending with misty eyes.

"I hardly dare look at you," Jimmie had said to her mother, after she'd shut off the set. "I know so well how skepticism sits on your brow."

"Sorry. I fear I'm not easily moved by fantasy."

"I'm not sure it's entirely fantasy," Mrs. Prior said. "At least, I'm not sure the *idea* is. A young man—Negro, at that, so young people of that class would have experiences in common with him—might work such a transformation. If he were as winning as Sidney Poitier, that is."

"Oh, my word, Mother. You can't even say something kind without sounding snobbish."

"Mother," Jimmie said quickly, to head them off before they could get into one of their genteel skirmishes, "*why* do we always have to look at the ugly *Is?* Why can't we be reminded now and then of what *could* be, in life? It's easy to laugh at a movie like this with its ginger peachy ending, but maybe you could do something harder—believe in its meaning. Maybe I mean its message. Here's this young teacher giving kids an idea of their own value, kids who didn't have any sense of it until he came along, and what better thing could a teacher do?"

"The children in the picture were in their middle or late teens, scarcely to be called children at all. If their sense of personal worth had been destroyed—well, there's no if about it, of course it had been destroyed—it had been done so long before that they'd be past having it restored in one year by a charismatic black."

"What did you say that time?" Jimmie asked. "That you've always believed in the ugliness of people? You meant it, didn't you?"

"I'm afraid I did."

"I'm sorry for you."

"Thank you. I think you mean that."

"Oh, believe me . . . I do."

"Now, as to throwing away the textbooks," Grandmother Prior had gone on thoughtfully, "I'm not sure he was altogether wise in doing that—"

Mrs. Gavin got up. "You'll excuse me. If you two are seriously going to discuss that sentimental claptrap, I'm going to bed."

"Good night, dear," said Mrs. Prior.

" 'Night, Mother," Jimmie said. "No, but Grandmother, don't you see that was one of the smartest things he did. I mean, like he said—"

"As he said."

"As he said—most of those kids couldn't *read*. What's the point of teaching South American geography to a bunch of kids who can barely make out the bus signs in their own town? He talked to them about life. And he let them talk. I mean, I think he was the greatest."

"The young man's a credit to his race, there's no question about that."

"Oh, Grandmother—" Jimmie burst out laughing. "You are too much."

But how funny, to be having fun talking with Grandmother Prior, she'd thought. And to be, in a way, almost talking about life.

That hadn't been the only time, either.

But they very rarely talked about Jimmie's mother, Grandmother's daughter, Mrs. Prior Gavin, as she now called herself. She, far from having a resurgence of the energy she'd shown that time in cleaning the house so she could get out of it, get rid of it, had retired further into her world of books, into her private rage at the world. A rage that could not stimulate her into activity but only drove her deeper into disgust and despair. Detached, much quieter, she spent her nights reading and her days resting and did not feel called upon to explain any more. Now, with Portia and Mr. Hunter, she didn't have to pretend to do housework. Jimmie, recalling that she'd once thought her mother might learn to drive a car, get a job, get *with it,* realized that had really been the stuff of fantasy. In a sense, her mother was easier to live with now.

Mrs. Gavin had arrived at her mother's house, had moved into the room she'd had as a girl, putting alongside her childhood books, which had been left on the shelves, her grown-up books of inquiry, philosophy, politics, anthropology—all those matters that fascinated her in print —had hung her three Chagall lithographs on the wall and then, giving her children into her mother's care, had abdicated. She had occasional listless disagreements with her mother, but on the whole she seemed to Jimmie to be a person whose thoughts, whose *being,* really, was always elsewhere. The people around her were like those wiggling lines that cross your vision, annoying but not really there.

One day Grandmother Prior, in an effort to draw her daughter out, or give her pleasure, had invited to the house for lunch two sisters who had known her when she'd been Elizabeth Prior, when they'd been girls together.

Jimmie, coming from school that day, had found her grandmother alone in the living room, sitting on a needlepoint chair that she and Goya were also allowed to sit on these days, if they exercised care. The chair had been worked by Grandmother's mother, and was beautiful.

"How'd it go, Grandmother?" Jimmie had asked.

Mrs. Prior had looked up, studying Jimmie's face. She'd beckoned her in.

"Was the lunch a success?" Jimmie asked, flopping on a sofa, then straightening. Grandmother didn't like people to sprawl.

"I think," Mrs. Prior said reflectively, "that your mother would have made a good religious, if she'd had a calling."

"Can you say a religious? I thought it was an adjective."

"Also a noun. Yes, your mother might well have made a life of contemplating life, if she'd had a vocation."

"So the lunch was a flop?"

"Aline Selwyn and Helen Salmon. The McIver girls, they were. Your mother now says she scarcely knew them, though that is not my recollection, or why would I have asked them here? They arrived promptly and had the look, somehow, of women who take cocktails before lunch. I hadn't thought of it until I saw them. Portia served sherry. Mrs. Selwyn has a habit of referring to herself by name. She says things like, 'Not for little Aline, *oh* no. Aline has to watch her calories.' She was not referring to the sherry but to Portia's Floating Island. She wore pants, jeans, I think. They were so tight she had to eat leaning against the wall."

"Oh, Grandmother." Jimmie giggled. "Not really."

"No. She managed to sit down. I can't think how. Mrs. Salmon is overweight and wore a mini skirt. Tasteless. Of course, I realize that women no longer wear dresses and gloves when they go calling, but these two are past teen-age clothes."

Grandmother had a way of labeling things as "teen-age," which was not, she said, pejorative.

"What's that?"

"Pejorative? It means derisive, depreciatory. But that is not the sense in which I say something is teen-age. I merely mean it descriptively. Some things are appropriate to those years, some things just are not."

Certain ways of dressing, talking, eating, were, to Grandmother, teen-age ways. Hot dogs, potato chips, cola drinks, candy bars were teen-age food. Looking at late shows or sleeping till noon were teen-age habits. Jimmie found that she didn't resent this attitude in her grandmother. She even approved of it, provided she wasn't prevented from eating hot dogs and looking at late shows now and then. And women in their thirties *were* past the age for tight jeans and mini skirts.

"So, what happened?" she said now.

"At first they simply fell upon your mother, speaking of 'olden times.' I realized immediately that the idea had been a mistake, that inviting these two young women, whom I recalled only as girls who'd known your mother, was ludicrous. After a while, they saw she was simply going through the motions of courtesy, so they talked to each other, and once in a while to me, during lunch. Your mother excused herself immediately afterward. She just walked out of the dining room, leaving me with her guests."

"Golly. Of course, they weren't really her guests, if you think it over. You invited them."

"Yes. I invited them," Mrs. Prior said dryly. "And I could see that your mother's need to escape took precedence over manners. Unfortunately, I could not escape."

"How long did they stay?"

"You may find this hard to credit, Janine, but they were here until nearly three o'clock, drinking sherry and telling me how Beth, my daughter, had always been a 'loner,' in school. 'Frightfully bright and all that, Mrs. P.'—they called me Mrs. P. the whole time '—but not

what you'd call the life of the party.'" Grandmother
Prior's voice took on a drunken slur as she quoted her
recent guests, and Jimmie had looked at her in admiration.

"You know, Mrs. P., I sometimes think you should've
been an actress."

"Really," said her grandmother, with an air of lofty
pleasure. "And how was your day, Janine?"

They discussed Jimmie's new school, forcing themselves
to forget the woman upstairs. What it comes to, Jimmie
thought sometimes, is that we have to think about her all
the time, and worry at her oddness, be frightened by it,
or we have to learn to live with her as she is.

Mrs. Prior did not make the mistake of inviting anyone
again to "draw her daughter out," and she and Jimmie accommodated to the strangeness of Mrs. Prior Gavin's life.
After all, Jimmie told herself, it's just a case of copping
out. Plenty of kids do it, so why shouldn't my mother?
Kids turn their backs on a society they fear and despise
and go to live in shacks in the woods. My mother's just
doing the same thing, only she's living in a museum. Trying to make two and two come out to five, or to three.

No, she corrected herself. She's living in a beautiful
house. Grandmother Prior's was no longer, to Jimmie, a
cold place, or a museum. And the reason was that Grandmother herself, making a tremendous effort, had been
the one who'd got with it.

She picked up her writing pad from the grass where it
had fallen. "If," she wrote, "I ever said that Grandmother's house is a museum, I take it back. Or, if it is, it's the
kind that has happenings in the gallery and do-it-yourself
art in the sculpture court—"

She dropped the pad to her lap and sighed. What a
dumb, affected letter. *Dear childhood friends*, for Pete's
sake.

She wanted to write as if nothing had changed, as if
separation had made no difference, and certainly it hadn't,
in her feelings for them, her affection. They were her
dearest friends and if she were *with* them, she knew it
would be as if no time had passed at all. She'd be able
to tell them how she felt, how her life was now. But she
couldn't write it.

She'd left, all those months ago—only a little over three? only that?—raging at her father, crying in Gram's arms, begging to live with her, whimpering to Chris about how cold Grandmother Prior was, how cold her house.

How did she write now that it wasn't that way at all? How had the change come about? She couldn't write it if she didn't understand it, if she only *knew* it. Writing it would take an essay, not a letter. Could she say that her stiff, chilly, unpleasable grandmother had undergone an epiphany and emerged fond and fun? It would sound patronizing. It would sound like sentimental claptrap. Yet it seemed to Jimmie that that was what had happened.

She looked at her grandmother, who was scanning the sky with her powerful binoculars, a smile on her lips.

"What do you see, Grandmother?"

"A brown-tailed hawk. So beautiful. Such a perfect creation. See how he glides on the air currents—" handing over the glasses to Jimmie.

Jimmie watched the great bird as he sailed across the sky, scarcely moving his wings. Oh yes, the brown-tailed hawk was perfect, and the wild geese were, and the towhees wrenching berries from the dogwood tree were perfect.

She gave the binoculars back and said, "Have you changed, or have I?"

Mrs. Prior did not pretend not to understand. She debated a moment. "Both of us, I daresay. We've tried to understand each other, and it's to our credit."

"But it's working. That's the part I didn't expect. I knew we'd *try*."

"Nor did I. Expect it. I'd hoped, of course."

"Were you afraid to have us here? Your beautiful house, your things—"

"I wanted you."

"I see. You've always seemed satisfied, the other way."

"I was very lonely."

"Oh."

One thing Jimmie had found was that she had to talk to someone about how she was feeling. It would have been fine to be reserved, self-contained, even a little mysterious, but it was not the way she was.

Mostly, in the past, she'd talked with her father or

Gram, or with her three friends. But she'd found that her mother would do—as on that stormy night in the kitchen —if her mother would listen. Which she mostly would not. Now, because her Grandmother Prior would listen, she talked to her.

"I'm always finding out discouraging things about myself," she said, not looking at her grandmother but at Mr. Hunter, who was digging up dahlia bulbs at the other end of the grassy lawn.

"Very likely. Those of us who take time to inquire into ourselves run into unedifying bits. Surely you find the opposite to be true, also?"

"Edifying bits? I guess so."

"Of course you do. People who do not find good and encouraging qualities in themselves are probably guilty of self-pity. It's a trait I've not observed much in you."

"Christina says her doctor says self-pity is the enemy."

"I'd agree. One of the enemies."

"Why didn't you ever like my father?"

Mrs. Prior caught her breath, then said as if meeting a challenge, "He never liked me."

"But you had things in common. Gardening. How could two people who love flowers so much not like each other?"

Grandmother Prior's eyes went over her garden and back to Jimmie. "Call it a personality clash. I don't know what else to say. Your father cast me in the role of snob. No doubt he'd call it typecasting, and no doubt he'd be right, to some extent."

"But you—you think being a dentist *is* sort of an inferior occupation. *Don't* you?"

"If I made—since I made—that impression, it was very wrong of me. People can't always help how they feel, but they should try to conceal feelings that are going to hurt others, I'm sorry, but I suppose I do feel that dentistry is —an odd profession to take up. I can't explain that, or defend it. I just react that way."

"Well," Jimmie said after a pause. "That's honest enough."

"We must be honest with each other, mustn't we?"

"Yes. We must."

They exchanged a glance both sympathetic and constrained. Jimmie was accustomed to speaking freely and personally to her other grandmother, but not to this one, and Mrs. Prior had lived so long alone, except for Portia, who had little to say to anyone and would not have her time imposed upon, that she'd long since fallen into the habit of silence.

They were relieved when Goya came into the garden with a cotton bag full of objects that they were going to be required to identify by feeling through the cloth. It was a game he'd learned in school and never tired of playing. Goya, indeed, was finding kindergarten a gas.

"Now," he said, planting himself in front of his grandmother. "Now, Gran, you feel first. I have four *objects* in here, and if you concentrate, you will be able to identify them."

He used the long words with confident pride. Goya had taken to calling his grandmother Gran, to her unexpressed delight. She hadn't called him George since they'd arrived.

Jimmie smiled and returned to her letter. Having got this far, she hated to waste the words, but there was nothing more she wanted, or knew how, to say about her life here. She'd talk to them about themselves. That was always welcome and unexpected in a letter.

CHAPTER TWENTY

She'd heard from all three of them—surprisingly from Marcy most of all. Early in the summer she had sent six postcards of the Unicorn tapestries from the Musée de Cluny in Paris. She'd written on just one. "It is impossible for me to say anything about these. I can only adore them, and hope one day you get to see them."

The postcards were so beautiful that Jimmie knew she'd have to be there one day, in the Cluny Museum, seeing them for herself. She wanted to stand for a long long time, seeking out every detail, seeing the little tapestried animals, the flowers and trees, and the white innocent delicate unicorn with its head on the maiden's lap.

Getting to Europe these days was a breeze, and cheap, and that was a thing to be said for the modern age. She'd manage.

She'd had another, later, postcard that Marcy had mailed from Rome. "Took the Blue Train from Florence to here. It is ROMANTIC. Red Turkish carpets, waiters with waxed eyelashes, jewel thieves, spies, and a Count who, I am sure, wished to make an assignation with me, only Mother wouldn't let me talk to anyone but our waiter. Little did she realize he could have been the most dangerous of the lot."

Jimmie had burst out laughing when she got this.

She'd had a note from Rome also.

"Went to the Protestant Cemetery here, to put a sprig

of rosemary on Keats' grave. It says on the tombstone, 'Here lies one whose name was writ on water.' That's all. A woman who was standing there said to her husband, 'I wonder why they don't say who it is.' No, really, that's true, she *did*. But she was unimportant and they went away, and I stayed there alone for a while. It reminded me, in a way, of Willow Farnham. Do you ever think of her? Of course, there's a chance that Willow was a peevish silly girl, passive, dull. That wouldn't have prevented her family from loving her, I suppose, and certainly wouldn't have prevented a 19c family from putting *Her family loved her, but Jesus loved her more* on her gravestone. But in my mind, Willow was lovely. I see her moving through her 16 years with a light nervous grace, and dying poetically. Is this a soppy note? It's meant to be moving, because I felt moved."

The last card had been mailed from London, the Beggs ladies' last stop. "By the time I got to Naples I'd found out that kissing is a two-way treat."

"I don't be*lieve* it," Jimmie muttered out loud. That was one postcard Mrs. Beggs had never seen before it got mailed.

Anne wrote from Castine that the water was too cold, as always, to swim in, but that she'd been doing a lot of sailing, much of it with Peter and a girl he'd brought up with him, named Rita Fortune. "Wouldn't you hate to go through life being addressed as 'Miss Fortune'? Well, maybe she'll get married. She's very attractive, if slightly actressy, and will never marry Peter as they like each other but have concluded they aren't in love. She's gone, now. Father had a ghastly time adjusting to what he quaintly called 'free love,' but Mother went along, except I think she's awfully relieved to have no more misfortune around. I asked Father if it wasn't better for people to find out about each other, whether they were suited and thought they could make a life together, before they did anything so drastic as getting married. He didn't answer. I think he agrees, because he, and everyone else, would have been miserable if Peter and Reeter had got married, but he couldn't bring himself to say so. Have you heard from Marcy? I can't say for sure, but I *think*, from the way she *writes,* that something extraordinary has happened to Marcy, and right under her mother's nose, too. By the way, speaking of abroad, Peter says that Dick Mosher has gone to Wales, maybe forever. How peculiar. I mean, it must be so bleak and Dylan Thomasy . . ."

So much, Jimmie had thought, for Anne's last year's love.

The notes from Anne and Marcy had been written when they still thought she was just visiting her Grandmother Prior. Later, they'd both written messages meant to sustain, and they had.

Christina had written a long letter after school started. "I write this from the study hall, where I should be doing tonight's homework, but got to thinking about you, so . . . Today is a gorgeously sunny snappy day into whose bright blue air I ventured at 7am, as I do every ayem now, because I've decided to bicycle to school. Cannot tolerate a year of that bus again. Now there isn't even Dick Mosher to take the curse off. He's gone to live in Wales, of all things. Anne took his departure with a stiff upper so-what. She's in love with the new chemistry teacher. He's twenty-five and tall and tan and rich and yummy. Rich, you'll understand, in things of the spirit, in a marvelous mustache, a good brain, a dear little fluffy wife and two children. You know, Marcy has always seemed the shy one (I'll get to her in a moment) but I've decided that Anne, for all that apparent independence, is maybe even more so. Probably for some time yet she'll fall madly in love with older, unattainable men to protect herself from the hazards of young & attainable ones. Which is okay, I guess. I saw a psychiatrist on the telly the other night, who said a thing of interest to you and me. He said that girls who have been deserted by their fathers tend to end up weirdos of one kind or another. Maybe that wasn't his *exact* term. He says whether the fathers die or desert or divorce them—I mean, divorce their mothers, of course—the girls in these cases grow up to be nymphos or homos or frigid or drunks or neurotics or actually nuts. That gives us quite a range of options, doesn't it." Gave my mother quite a range, too, Jimmie had thought. Her mother had, apparently, settled for neurosis. Or neurosis had settled for her. "Just the same," Chris had gone on, "I've decided not to opt for any of the options. I opt to be a sane and sober and probably unemployed female engineer. The unforeseen development of the summer, of course, is Marcy, who went slumping off to Europe a pale wick of a woman and returned a FLAME, to whom (to which?) moth males are already fluttering. She told us, Anne and me, and she'll tell you when you come down (when are you coming by the way? Aren't you going to visit your father? I saw him with his new wife downtown last week, and she looks very nice, Jimmie, *really*. She looks loving, which is what a man needs, so don't be too hard on him. Fathers don't grow on *trees*, you know). Back to Marcy—she met this young man in Florence when she was trying to find the American Express side of the Arno. He's shorter than she is but she said he absolutely insisted she straighten up and be TALL. He said, she says, that since he'd had the good, the glorious, fortune to meet a girl from a Botticelli canvas, then she must *walk* like a girl from a Botticelli canvas. That's what she says he said, and I believe her. He kissed her in Florence, when her mother thought she was culture-sopping at the Pitti Palace, kissed her in Rome (where he *followed* her!) in the Borghese Gardens, when her mother was at Elizabeth Arden's and thought Marcy was getting to know Rome, which as a matter of fact, she was, only not on the tour bus, and followed her to Naples and Sorrento, & I didn't find out what her mother thought she was doing then & am not absolutely sure what Marcy and Lino were doing besides kissing, as she delicately declined further details and quite right of her, too. She looks lovely and gets mail from him at my house. Now, of course, you're dying to know about me. Me. Well, I'm still struggling in the Laocoön embrace of my Encounter Group and confidently expect that one day—probably the day I get away from home for good, which makes it a little less than three years to go—I'll have the old tête in order. Write to us. But don't use long words like pejorative again. It shakes my self-confidence. Do you have any friends? Girl friends? Boyfriends? How's school and your mother and your grandmother and Goya? Let me say, in

the event that you have not deduced it, we miss you. So
WRITE."

I miss them, Jimmie thought. But somehow the days
went by and she'd find that another had passed during
which she'd not taken the time to write them, and the
more days went by, the more she thought how impossible it would be to catch up in a letter, until by the beginning of December it seemed hopeless.

She'd just have to wait until she saw them. Only, when
would that be? She could visit any one of them any time
she chose, but that would mean being in the town with
her father and his wife and she was not ready, she never
would be ready, to face that.

Did she have any friends? Girl friends, boyfriends?
Grandmother would not countenance the use of those
terms. She had some friends who were girls. Not the sort
of friends she'd had in Chris and Anne and Marcy. But
she'd known them since she'd been a kid Goya's age, practically. She'd probably never have friends like that again.
She missed them. And she missed Gram. And she hadn't
seen any of them for months and didn't write, not even to
Gram. She was ashamed of herself, sometimes almost
panicky, at how she let the days and weeks go by and
did not write.

She said something about it to her mother one day, and
Mrs. Prior Gavin, with her uncanny way of selecting the
appropriate quotation, had offered her Emily Brontë's:
*Surer than that dwelling dread, the narrow dungeon of
the dead, time parts the hearts of men.*

"Oh, golly," Jimmie had said miserably, from a real
sense of guilt and neglect. "That's horrible."

"Isn't it. But true, I'm afraid. We move away from people vowing we can't be without them, promising to write,
to visit, to telephone, to *keep in touch.* And then the need
for them lessens, and then if we remember them at all,
it's just with a little rue. Nothing much more."

"I don't believe it."

"Good for you."

That afternoon she wrote a long letter to Gram in
Michigan, telling about Goya's joy in kindergarten, and
about some girls she'd met and got along with quite well,

and about her classes, all of which she liked, and how good it was to be able to walk to school instead of riding a school bus, and how pretty the countryside was—a dull dull letter, which she ended by saying how she missed her Gram, loved her, missed her, loved her . . .

She said nothing about her father, didn't mention her Grandmother Prior or her mother, didn't ask about Christmas that was coming. Her father, she assumed, would go to Michigan with his new wife to be with "the family," of which she and her mother and Goya were no longer a part.

It would be the very first Christmas of her life that she had not been with her father.

Well, she'd survive that, too.

There was an ever present, sometimes muted, pain that lay across her life, her spirits. She thought to herself that it was like some beaked bright bird in a muffled cage that nevertheless managed to dart its head through the bars and stab at her. One of her crazy metaphors again, but this one seemed cruelly real. Missing her father made her restless, snappish. Even her new-found companionship with her Grandmother Prior was sometimes strained by her short temper, and only Grandmother's new-found— long temper?—saved them at those times.

"Grandmother?" Her voice aggressive, so that Mrs. Prior looked up warily. "Do you believe in God?"

"I go to church."

"That wasn't what I asked."

"No, it wasn't. Well—I do not believe in a deity who thinks, who broods over man and his difficulties, who attends to prayers, and plots punishments and pleasures for the afterlife. I do not believe in the afterlife."

"You're telling me what you don't believe in. I want to know what you *do*."

"It's almost impossible to answer that."

"I would appreciate it if you'd try. It's important to me."

Grandmother Prior's brow furrowed, but briefly. Guarding against wrinkles, Jimmie thought, aware of her own meanness and unable to subdue it.

"Perhaps you could call me a pantheist," her grandmother said.

"Perhaps I could, if I knew what it was."

"Pantheism—it's a system of belief which holds that God is not *somebody*. God is all. God is the universe, and its laws, the *whole*, but not an all-powerful, anthropomorphic being. A pantheistic God is not *concerned* with human beings or anything else. It just is, as the universe is, or an atom is. I couldn't believe in an orthodox church God, because then I'd have to believe him evil, since he'd be permitting mankind to be what mankind is. Perhaps you could call me an animist. I do believe in Nature, and that godliness is in the coming into leaf of trees in the spring, in the fact that birds sing and soar and build their nests, and we can hear and see them. There is so much that's beautiful in our world, and I think there is good, and perhaps God, in that."

"Do pantheists and animists go to Episcopal churches?"

Mrs. Prior smiled wryly. "I fear they have no churches, as such. And I go to church, Janine, because I find the ritual, and the music, in some way soothing to my spirit. And because I think many of the congregation are trying, at least during that hour, during the service, to know what good is. I go because our minister, Dr. Mears, is a good kind man and needs attendance."

"I see. Well, I think I'll start going with you. I don't believe in God at all, you understand, but I need some sort of *order* to my life. Something soothing for my spirit, I guess."

"I'll be happy to have you."

Dr. Mears, the minister, had a son, Julian, who was sixteen and a nonconformist, as Jimmie said to her mother, the afternoon after she'd met him.

"Nonconformist how?"

"He wears his hair short and has a suit with a jacket and pants that match and a tie. He wore them to church. And he helps his parents around the house."

"Good heavens, he is out of step. How old is he?"

"Sixteen. He has a car."

"Oh, really. Young people. They make such a clamor about rejecting the hypocrisies of their elders, but what about their own hypocrisies? Dad, I'm off to Vermont to eat seeds and lead the simple life but I'll need Head skis and a Porsche and some Austrian hiking boots to get me started—"

"I suppose there are hypocrisies at any age. And confusions about goals and how to reach them. I mean, aren't there?"

"Yes. You're right, of course. Parents don't help much. They buy kids too much. We do, I mean. I'm a parent, too," she conceded, and then smiled when Jimmie did. "Just the same. And this boy is a minister's son, too. You'd think he'd have been given a better sense of values. Of course, traditionally, ministers' sons are notorious scapegraces."

"I don't think Julian is the scapegrace type. And his car is nearly as old as he is."

She'd met him at the Young Communicants' Class, which she'd decided to attend, because as long as she was going to church she might as well go all the way and find out, if she could, what it was all about, if it was about anything.

The young assistant minister, whom everybody called by his first name, Dave, had led a discussion about the Book of Genesis and how they were to interpret "a day," in the Biblical sense. Was it a twenty-four-hour day? A billion-hour day? What was meant by, "On the seventh day he rested"? And what, then, of the Garden of Eden— had it been an actual place or a time of innocence remembered or imagined? Jimmie had found her attention wandering, and then it had snapped back again when Dave said that he'd like, at their next meeting, to try out "body movements to the Old Testament."

She'd gone out of the meeting room alone, rather perplexed. Today's discussion, in which all but she had taken part—in which, apparently, all but she had taken pleasure, had been a bore. Not a super-bore. Just a talky, everyday bore. But that about body movements to the Old Testament, what about that? If there hadn't been so many people crowding around Dave—he was awfully popular—she might have asked, but it didn't seem worth the bother, so she just cut out and started home.

Julian Mears caught up with her at the end of the

block and said, "You weren't much taken with that, were you?"

She turned, flushed a little when she saw who it was. The minister's son, wouldn't you know. "I'm sorry," she said. "I didn't mean to offend anybody."

"Oh, nobody takes offense in our church."

"My goodness. Are you sure?"

"I meant—nobody gets uptight over dogma and things. We like to think we can embrace all kinds of thinking and believing, and even nonbelieving."

"In a church?"

"In a church."

"Are you going to be a minister, too?"

"I haven't ruled it out, yet."

He'd fallen into step beside her.

"I live nearly a mile away," she cautioned him. "I mean —I didn't mean that you were—" again she was blushing "—I didn't mean you were going to walk home with me. I only meant—"

"Well, I'll go along a way. Do you walk every day? Both ways?"

"Unless it's pouring. It's self-therapy. I'm trying to get my head together, in a less violent way than a friend of mine is getting hers—assembled."

"Yours is disassembled?"

"Whose isn't?"

He nodded, and they walked in silence for a while. "I'm Julian Mears," he said in a bit.

"I know. I'm—I'm Janine Gavin."

"I know that. Your grandmother has been coming to the church ever since my father took over. I used to be afraid of her."

"Why?"

"She was awfully stern and starched. I always got the feeling, if her glance happened to fall on me, that I looked and sounded pretty tacky. But my father explained to me that lonely people often get that way." He stopped. "Now I've put my foot in it again. Sorry."

"I know my grandmother was starchy and stern. I know she was lonely. It was sort of her own fault. But she's better now. Since we came to live here, I mean. She likes having us." Aware they were heading toward some sort of explanation of her situation here, of her mother's divorce, Jimmie said hastily, "How often does the Young Communicants' Class meet?"

"Nothing regular about it. When we have time, or a holiday, or when something comes up we feel like talking about. You weren't fascinated by today's discussion, were you?"

"Not really. No matter how much time you assign to a day, I still believe in evolution."

"God and evolution aren't mutually exclusive."

Evolution and Genesis are, thought Jimmie, but ruled it out as rude to say to a minister's son, no matter how many kinds of belief and nonbelief his church could embrace.

"What's that about body movements to the Old Testament?" she asked.

"Oh, it's sort of fun. You interpret parts of the Bible with pantomime or dance or gestures or shouts—any way you feel like interpreting them. We enacted the flight of the Jews from Egypt last time, using those marvelous steps from *Fiddler on the Roof*—they're traditional Hebrew dance steps. We added some of our own, making them up as we went along. That's therapy, too, in a way."

"Well, I guess I'll try that. I mean, I'll keep coming to the class."

"Good."

They walked in silence, the bright air cold against their cheeks. Leaving the town behind, they crossed a bridge and started up the long hill that led to Mrs. Prior's.

"Now, if I had my car," Julian said, "I'd be driving you home. Not exactly in style, but in—well, in my car."

"Gee, you have a car? Where is it?"

"In the Intensive Care Unit of the local service station, having a carburetor transplant."

"Oh, dear. Is there hope for some hope?"

"It's critical, of course. But getting the best of care. Mechanics around the clock."

"Well, I do hope it'll be all right."

"Oh, so do I. My older brother buried a car last week, and we don't want another funeral like that in the family for some time."

Jimmie turned her head and scrutinized him carefully.

"No, really," Julian said. "He did. It's a very sad and pretty long story. Care to hear it?"

"I'll stay for the beginning, anyway."

"Okay. Well—my brother, Andy, had these two cars he picked up, one from a junkyard and one somebody gave him. One had a body, sort of, but no engine. I mean, there was a motor in there, but it was past reclamation. The other had an engine, but no body to speak of. No wheels, even. They were in the driveway of the parish house for weeks. Drove my mother up the walls."

"That's odd."

Julian grinned. "Anyway. So, Andy and I and some friends of ours spent all our spare time last summer trying to meld the pretty good engine with the pretty good body. It's hairy work, especially if you don't know anything about cars. Andy and I don't. We've got a lot of ideas about naming cars, but no idea how they run."

"What about naming them?"

"Well, you have to grant that the motor industry in this country is copping out on this business of characterizing their product. Wildcat, Cutlass, Barracuda—sissy stuff. Andy and I'd lay the facts on them. We're going to write to G.M. and tell them to name their next model ASSASSIN. What do you think of that?"

"I think I won't ride in your car, even if it does recover."

"Oh, mine's named Inertia. Nobody need be afraid of her. Except afraid she won't go, of course."

"Go on about getting the body and the mind—I mean, engine—together. If you don't know anything about cars, how did you do it?"

"Determination is a factor. And a friend of ours who's sort of mechanical—it's not his strongest point, but he knows more than we do, anyway—came along to lend us a hand, and lots of kibitzers showed and offered advice and even some muscle. We got it done. Took nearly four months."

"Your poor mother."

"But then we had this engineless corpse on our hands, in the driveway, and no one would take it away. We tried everything, and finally offered money if someone would just get it out of there."

"That should've been the first thing you did."

"We thought we could sell it for junk."

"You know something," Jimmie said, enjoying this walk, this talk, more than she dared show, "I've never owned a car, with or without wheels or an engine, and I'm not mechanical, and I can't imagine a situation like that arising, but if it ever should arise, I am absolutely confident I wouldn't expect to sell a piece of junk like that for junk. How did the one without wheels get to the parish house driveway to begin with?"

"It had wheels when it came. A friend of ours, the mechanical one, towed it over for us, and his payment *was* the wheels. We never stopped to think what a problem the thing was going to be without them."

"Some friend. So, then what happened?"

"I'm coming to that. To the burial. First we thought, when we realized that nobody was going to take it away for us, and Mom was getting flushed and feverish every time she looked out the window and asking us to *do* something—well, the first thing we tried was to saw it up. We thought we'd saw it in little pieces and bury them. But we broke Dad's chain saw, the very first whack—"

Jimmie burst out laughing. She was so happy she wanted to shout, but laughing would do.

"—and that's when we decided to bury the whole darn thing. It was right at the edge of the driveway, so we started digging a hole beside it in the lawn. Do you have a notion how long it takes to dig a grave for something as big as a car?"

"Nope."

"Takes too long. We'd be digging yet, except that our friend, the mechanical one, had a friend with a little bulldozer, and he brought it over one afternoon and scooped out a big enough hole and then we all got together—the place was milling with onlookers, you'd think nobody had ever seen a car buried before—and pushed it into the hole. Boy, it was some moment," he said in a tone of relish. "We threw in an old stove that had been in the garage for ages waiting for someone to take it away—you can't get anything taken away these days—and one of the neighbors put her broken dishwasher in, and people threw some other junk they wanted to get rid of in, and then we covered it all over and planted grass seed on the plot. Andy wanted to put a headstone with RIP on it, but Dad wouldn't let him."

Jimmie sighed with pleasure and realized that the mile had been walked. They were at her grandmother's gate. "This is where I live."

"Yeah, I know." He studied the big house. "Beautiful, isn't it? The sign says it was built in 1809. They really built in those days, didn't they?"

"I love it," Jimmie said. It was not a museum, not cold. It was her home. It was a beautiful house, and she loved it.

"Want some hot chocolate, or something?" she asked.

Julian hesitated. "I should be getting back. I told my mother I'd wax the kitchen floor for her."

Jimmie tried to cover her look of surprise, but didn't.

"None of that 'He's a boy so don't let him get his hands in dishwater,' for my mother. Andy and I have been worked like slaves since we fell out of the cradle," he said without resentment.

"You could have some chocolate and then ride my bike back to town."

"Hey, okay. That sounds swell."

Mrs. Prior was in the morning room and they joined her there after making hot chocolate in the kitchen. She had some with them, and talked pleasantly with Julian.

"I'm sorry you can't meet my daughter, Janine's mother. She's resting. But perhaps some other time. You'll come to see us again, I hope."

"I sure will," said Julian, with a glance at Jimmie that seemed to arrest her heartbeat.

Jimmie wrote to her three friends one evening a week or so later, after she'd done her homework and washed her hair and made sure that what she was going to wear the next day was pretty and had all the buttons on.

"Dearest Anne, Christina, and Marcy: You'll be surprised, maybe, and, I trust, delighted to learn that I have a—" she hesitated, wrote "—a friend who is a boy. His name is Julian Mears and he's the minister here's son—I mean, the son of the Episcopal minister here, and he's kind of square and absolutely marvelous. How I met him, was—"

CHAPTER TWENTY-ONE

On Christmas Eve, Goya, before going to bed, said he was going to get some milk and cookies to leave on the hearth for Santa Claus.

Mrs. Prior Gavin, Mrs. Prior, and Jimmie exchanged glances and sighed. All at once, with an air of plunging, Mrs. Gavin said to her son, "Goya, drink the milk and eat the cookies yourself."

Jimmie gasped, and Grandmother Prior caught her lower lip in her strong white teeth.

Goya looked at his mother in astonishment, and Jimmie said, "Mom, please—"

"I'm sorry. But this just can't go on. Is he going to be putting out repasts for Father Christmas when he's twenty? I mean, when *do* we break the news to him? When he starts shaving? Goya," she said, "listen to me, please. The fact, Goya, is this—Santa Claus doesn't actually come down the chimney with a bag of toys, and he doesn't ride his sleigh through the sky on Christmas Eve, or live at the North Pole either. In fact, Goya, Santa Claus is like a beautiful story that we tell ourselves for pleasure, not for believing in. It's like any of the stories that Jimmie reads to you. You don't think Jemima Puddleduck is real, do you?" Her son didn't answer, but regarded her face attentively, with some puzzlement. "Well, anyway—try to understand. All children, at some time in their lives, have to face the truth, which is that Santa Claus simply isn't there. So, no milk and cookies, do you understand?"

He sat down, looking from one to the other of his grown-ups. "When are you going to do the tree?" he asked.

At least he doesn't think Santa Claus does that, Jimmie said to herself, and answered, "After you've gone to bed, love. So really, it's up to you."

He jumped to his feet. "Think I'll go to bed." He kissed his mother on the cheek, turned to his grandmother. "You coming, Gran?"

"After Janine puts you to bed, I'll be up to say good night. Maybe I can read the story tonight."

Goya nodded. "It's *The Tailor of Gloucester*. It's about Christmas Eve."

"I know. I'll be up."

"Where's Portia?" Goya asked.

"She's gone home, to spend the holiday with her family."

"I made her a present. It's—" He stopped in time, remembering that he'd made the same thing for his mother, his grandmother, and Jimmie. Small clay bowls, painted and glazed and fired in the school oven. Jimmie had helped him wrap them, not looking at her own. Remembering her own homemade presents in the far past, she knew how he was itching with anticipation of the moment when the wrappings would be torn away and the splendor of his offerings revealed.

"Come on, Goya," she said. "Sooner to bed, sooner to rise." Probably at five, she thought, and since she and her grandmother were going to midnight mass, it didn't look like a long winter's nap for them.

In his room, in his pajamas, in his bed, Goya looked at his sister and said calmly, "I guess Santa Claus gets things to eat at every house, practically, don't you think? So he won't be hungry when he gets here."

Jimmie stared at him, groped for something to say, and failed entirely. Apparently Goya would relinquish his beliefs and fantasies at his own, and at no one else's, pace.

Well, there was one thing she, herself, would not do, and that was go along anymore with his dancing scarecrows, his witches, and wandering snowmen. If he per-

sisted in having St. Nicholas cruise the sky on Christmas
Eve, he was going to have to carry on alone from here.

She leaned over to kiss his forehead, taking a moment
to wish that the porcelain complexion of little children
never went away. So now I've started, she thought wryly.
Same as Anne, same as Grandmother. Embarked on woman's lifelong contention with the forces of age. All because of a boy? Probably all because of a boy.

"Pleasant dreams, darling."

"Pleasant dreams, Jimmie." He was the only one left,
besides herself, in her mind, who still called her Jimmie.
He smiled at her happily and snuggled under the covers to
wait for his grandmother, and preparing, no doubt, to
listen for sleigh bells with the calm confidence of a true
believer.

When Grandmother Prior had gone upstairs, Jimmie
and her mother began to decorate the big tree. They were
looping yards of cranberry ropes and popcorn strings
over thick fragrant branches, when Grandmother came
back into the morning room, looking bemused. Jimmie
grinned as their eyes met and Grandmother lifted hers to
the ceiling. In the way they had arrived at of tacitly understanding each other, they said nothing of Goya's res-
olute suspension of disbelief.

Jimmie rummaged in a box of ornaments and came up
with the swan with its tarnished tinsel tail, and, in the
same tissue wrapping, two of the tiny birds with wire legs
that her father had carved and painted long ago.

She was absolutely unprepared for the wave of physical pain and longing that rushed at her, washed over her,
tumbling her senses, blurring her vision, deafening her.
Daddy! she cried silently. Where are you? Where is my
father? I want my *father* . . .

She felt, in a little while, her mother's hand on her
shoulder, heard her mother's voice cry, "Jimmie! Jimmie,
what's the matter? Are you sick?"

She straightened, swallowing painfully. "Janine, remember?" was all she could think to say.

Mrs. Gavin's hand fell away, and her face, on which
Jimmie had got a picture of suffering and concern, was at
once passive again.

"Of course. Janine. I thought you were sick, you doubled over so suddenly."

"Just a cramp. I'm fine." She met her grandmother's eye and repeated, "I'm fine."

In bed that night, after the midnight mass to which she and Grandmother had been driven by Mr. Hunter, who also attended, she lay awake, still hearing the organ music, the singing, seeing the candles and the white and gold of the altar, remembering the look in Julian's eyes as they searched for her and brightened when he saw her. He'd given her a little package as she and Grandmother left the church, slipping it into her hand with a, "Merry first Christmas, Janine."

She saw, and remembered, and heard all that in her mind, but it was not what mattered to her now. She remembered, felt, endured again, out of the whole evening, that fleeting sight of her mother's face, on which there had been pain and appeal, erased in a moment.

Because I didn't respond, Jimmie thought, feeling a sadness worse because the next time, if there should be a next time, she would do the same. How we hurt each other, when we don't want to, she thought painfully, almost angrily. We hurt each other when because of what went before there is nothing we can do but hurt each other.

Oh, it is too hard, *living*. She rolled to her stomach, her face in the pillow. It's too *hard* on people, and how do they ever get through it?

She cried, for the release that tears bring. Cried for her mother and her father, for her grandmothers and for poor Faith Powers, for Goya who had to grow up and lose his beautiful delusions. She thought she was crying for everyone she had ever known, and for herself, and for all the world except Willow Farnham who had not known pain for a hundred years now, and more. You really could envy Willow Farnham, who'd got it all over with.

She fell asleep, and then Goya was waking her up, pulling the pillow off her head, shaking her by the arm.

"Jimmie, it's snowing!"

She'd known it was. It had started before midnight.

Now it was sifting up the corners of the windowpanes and outside it was falling thickly.

It was Christmas again, and snowing. She threw her arms around her brother and held him. "Goya, you did it!" she said, holding him so tight that he wriggled in her arms. "Merry Christmas, darling."

In the afternoon, in her new crushed grape cashmere sweater (from Grandmother), with her gold enameled butterfly brooch (from her mother) pinned to it, and Julian's thin beaten silver bracelet around her wrist, she sat on the floor amid the Christmas litter looking at a little set of carved wooden trains. Her mother and Grandmother were in the kitchen, getting dinner. Goya was out in the snow on his new sled, and had left the trains here on the floor of the morning room. There were five cars, an engine, and a caboose. There was a set of tracks, a little station house, a tiny tree, and a minute cow looking over a length of wooden fence. Looming over the cow, seeming to look down on the whole scene, was a fox, her fox, who wasn't really big at all, only in relation to Goya's train set. Her father never made animals cute, never made them look partway human. This was entirely a fox, with fragile legs and a pointed face and a full but slender tail. He was buffed to a high shine and had one front paw lifted. His face was turned a little to the side, as if he were listening, listening—

He must have stopped work on the chess set as soon as he left the old house, Jimmie thought. He must have worked on the trains, the little station house, the tiny cow, and the beautiful little fox all during these months when we haven't written to him or spoken to him. She closed her eyes, trying to picture him. He'd be sitting in a room she could not picture. But he, her father, was clear enough. He wore his old tan button-down sweater and handled the dentist's drill, the sharp thin tools, carefully, delicately, as he worked on Christmas presents for his children whom he didn't see or hear from, but loved. But loved.

Jimmie forced the presence of Emily Copeland into this picture, but somehow she did not seem menacing. She did not seem anything. She did not even seem there, though it was sure enough she was.

Only not for me, not now, Jimmie thought. There was no one in her mind's picture but her father, patiently carving a little fox, a set of little trains.

"Christmas afternoon is a drag," she said aloud, "and it always has been." Trying to put the blame for how she felt on the day, and the time of the day. But it wouldn't work because it wasn't that.

She got up, walked to the telephone in the hall, and dialed a number in Michigan. She knew it well enough from having called Gram there in the long ago past. Her mother and Grandmother might hear her, but that was all right. She stood, poised as though on a springboard, tense, trembling a little, hearing the telephone ring in the house in Michigan she had never seen, where Gram was, where her father maybe was. Would he be there? Where was he? Who would answer the telephone? Would anyone answer at all?

The ringing went on, and then was cut off, and Jimmie, who could hold her breath no longer, let it out in a long sigh as she heard her father's voice. Dear, resonant, beloved voice—

"Hello?" he said.

"Daddy—Daddy, this is Janine."

"At last George Plimpton has been out Plimptoned.
Gloria Steinem has met her match.
Joe Namath can retire and rest his sore knees."

HAL HIGDON

Zanballer

R. R. KNUDSON

Suzanne Hagen wanted nothing to do with cheer-
leading, baton twirling or folkdancing. She wanted
to play ball; and if boys could play football, why
not girls? Zan's remarkable gridiron career began
when her principal closed down the gym for re-
pairs and forced the girls to participate in such
unsporting activities as folk dancing. In revolt,
Zan led them out of dance class and onto the football field, where they formed a team called Catch-
11 and began their uphill run to football glory.

A LAUREL-LEAF LIBRARY BOOK 95¢
8819-04

Laurel-Leaf Library for young adult readers

Outstanding Laurel-Leaf Fiction for Young Adult Readers

☐ **A LITTLE DEMONSTRATION OF AFFECTION**
Elizabeth Winthrop $1.25
A 15-year-old girl and her older brother find themselves turning to each other to share their deepest emotions.

☐ **M.C. HIGGINS THE GREAT**
Virginia Hamilton $1.25
Winner of the Newbery Medal, the National Book Award and the Boston Globe-Horn Book Award, this novel follows M.C. Higgins' growing awareness that both choice and action lie within his power.

☐ **PORTRAIT OF JENNY**
Robert Nathan $1.25
Robert Nathan interweaves touching and profound portraits of all his characters with one of the most beautiful love stories ever told.

☐ **THE MEAT IN THE SANDWICH**
Alice Bach $1.25
Mike Lefcourt dreams of being a star athlete, but when hockey season ends, Mike learns that victory and defeat become hopelessly mixed up.

☐ **Z FOR ZACHARIAH**
Robert C. O'Brien $1.25
This winner of an Edgar Award from the Mystery Writers of America portrays a young girl who was the only human being left alive after nuclear doomsday—or so she thought.